THE BOND

Manuel Pelaez

The Bond by Manuel Pelaez

978-1-955136-89-1 (Paperback)

Printed in the United States of America
New Leaf Media, LLC
175 S. 3rd Street, Suite 200
Columbus, OH 43215
www.thenewleafmedia.com

INTRODUCTION

I create fantastical realms that are beyond imagination, filled with extraordinary dreams and the narratives that give them substance. It brings me immense joy to captivate audiences worldwide by infusing vibrant hues, compelling characters, intense emotions, and sublime humor into tales of unparalleled fantasy. In this particular epic novel, I explore the magnificence and abundant treasures hidden within the enigmatic depths of the underwater realm.

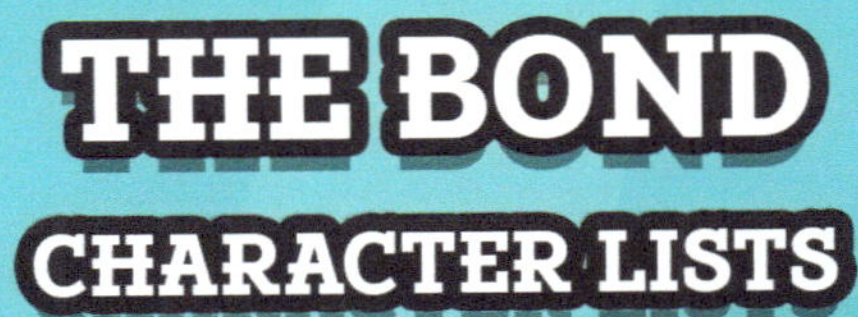

THE BOND
CHARACTER LISTS

FINN (the magical blue throat trigger fish)

JEREMY (main character)

LEAH (daughter fo Royal Family)

RAYMOND (Jeremy's father and Lieutenant of the US Navy)

CAROLE (Jeremy's mom)

CAROLE's MOM

THE ROYAL FAMILY

GREAT SAMURAI

THE OCTOPUS UNDERWATER SYMPHONY ORCHESTRA

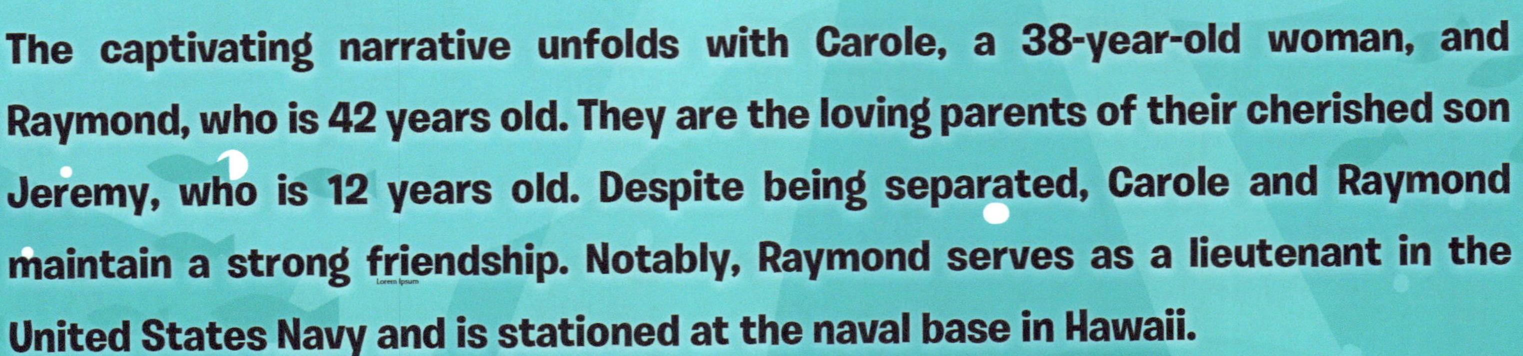

The captivating narrative unfolds with Carole, a 38-year-old woman, and Raymond, who is 42 years old. They are the loving parents of their cherished son Jeremy, who is 12 years old. Despite being separated, Carole and Raymond maintain a strong friendship. Notably, Raymond serves as a lieutenant in the United States Navy and is stationed at the naval base in Hawaii.

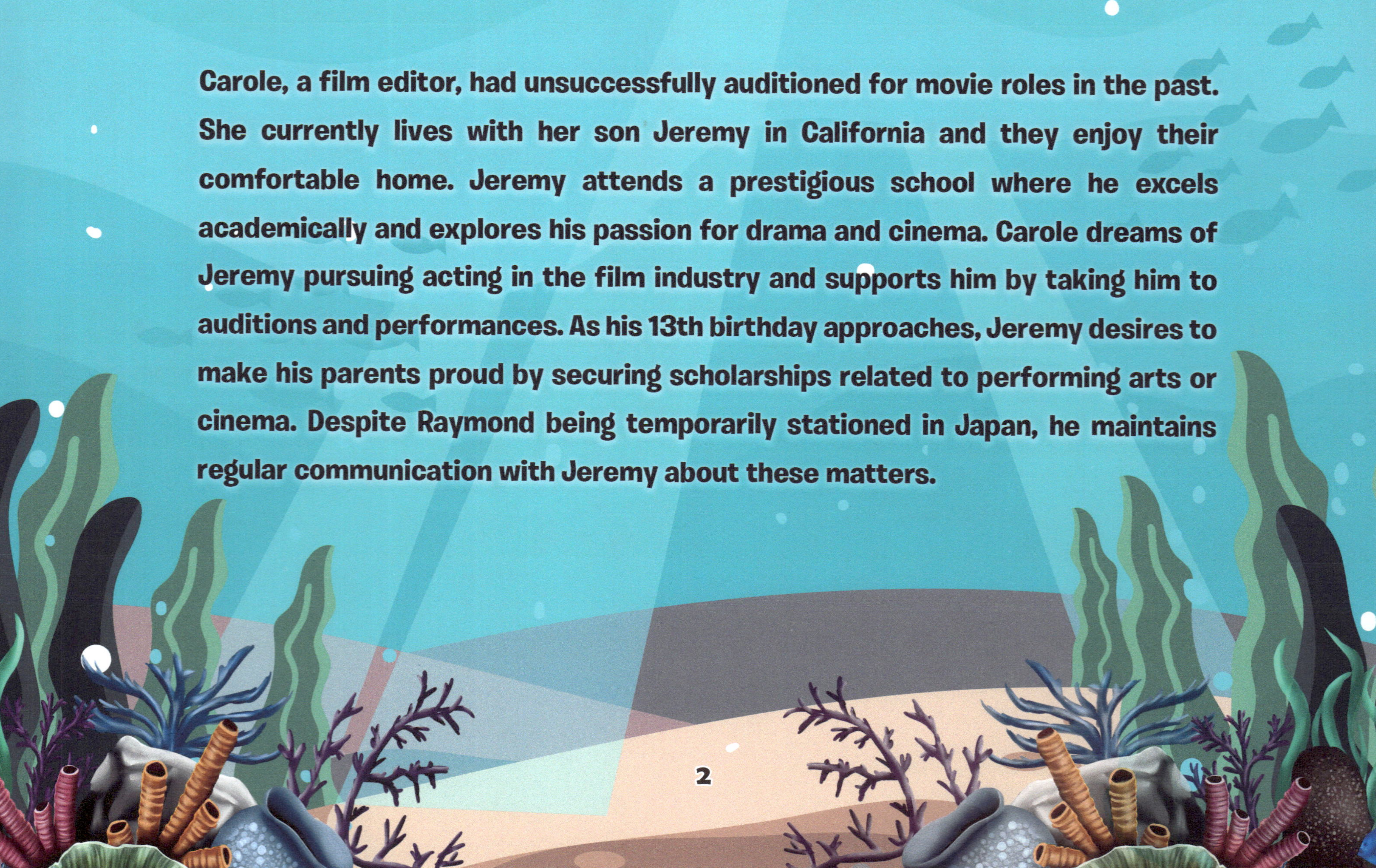

Carole, a film editor, had unsuccessfully auditioned for movie roles in the past. She currently lives with her son Jeremy in California and they enjoy their comfortable home. Jeremy attends a prestigious school where he excels academically and explores his passion for drama and cinema. Carole dreams of Jeremy pursuing acting in the film industry and supports him by taking him to auditions and performances. As his 13th birthday approaches, Jeremy desires to make his parents proud by securing scholarships related to performing arts or cinema. Despite Raymond being temporarily stationed in Japan, he maintains regular communication with Jeremy about these matters.

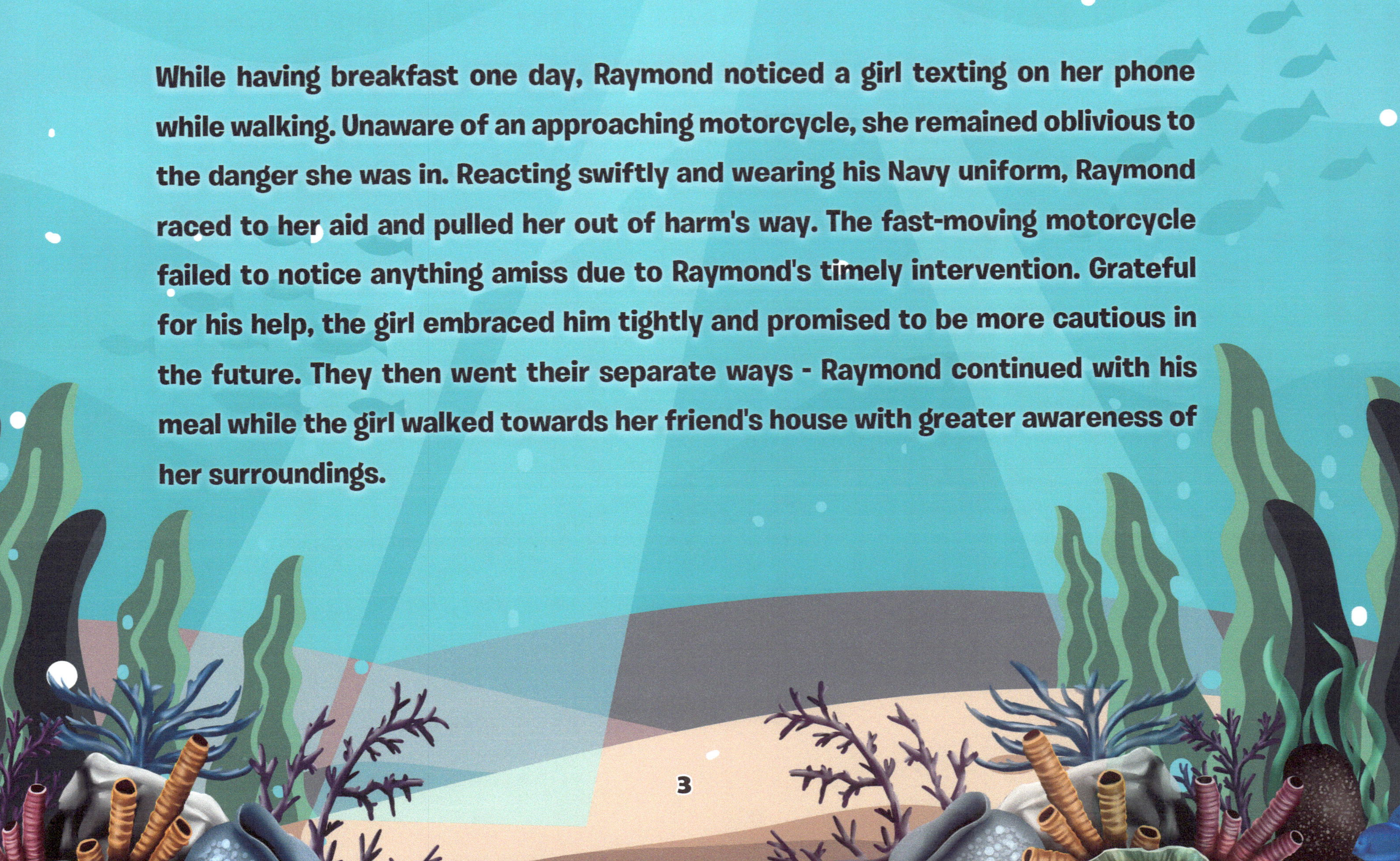

While having breakfast one day, Raymond noticed a girl texting on her phone while walking. Unaware of an approaching motorcycle, she remained oblivious to the danger she was in. Reacting swiftly and wearing his Navy uniform, Raymond raced to her aid and pulled her out of harm's way. The fast-moving motorcycle failed to notice anything amiss due to Raymond's timely intervention. Grateful for his help, the girl embraced him tightly and promised to be more cautious in the future. They then went their separate ways - Raymond continued with his meal while the girl walked towards her friend's house with greater awareness of her surroundings.

Raymond unknowingly came across Leah, the 13-year-old daughter of Japan's royal family. The incident was witnessed by their close friends and neighbors who maintain a strong bond with the royals. Word spread rapidly when Leah returned home and confirmed the event to her parents upon questioning.

The following day, Lieutenant Raymond is invited by the royal family to a dinner held at their palace, where he is welcomed as an esteemed guest. Dressed in his pristine white naval uniform, Lt. Raymond garners admiration and respect from those stationed at the Naval base. Throughout the course of dinner within the exquisite temple surroundings, expressions of appreciation and gratitude are extended to him by members of the royal family.

After dinner, Raymond is given a special gift from the royal family - an aquarium with a beautiful blue throat triggerfish. He expresses his gratitude and mentions his son's upcoming birthday, stating how much he will cherish this unique present. Raymond also appreciates being invited to their palace and acknowledges the value of saving their daughter from a reckless motorcyclist, which will make her more cautious when crossing roads in the future. These events strengthen our bond and ensure lifelong friendship between both families. Accompanied by an escort back to the naval base, Raymond eagerly looks forward to sharing this wonderful news with his son Jeremy.

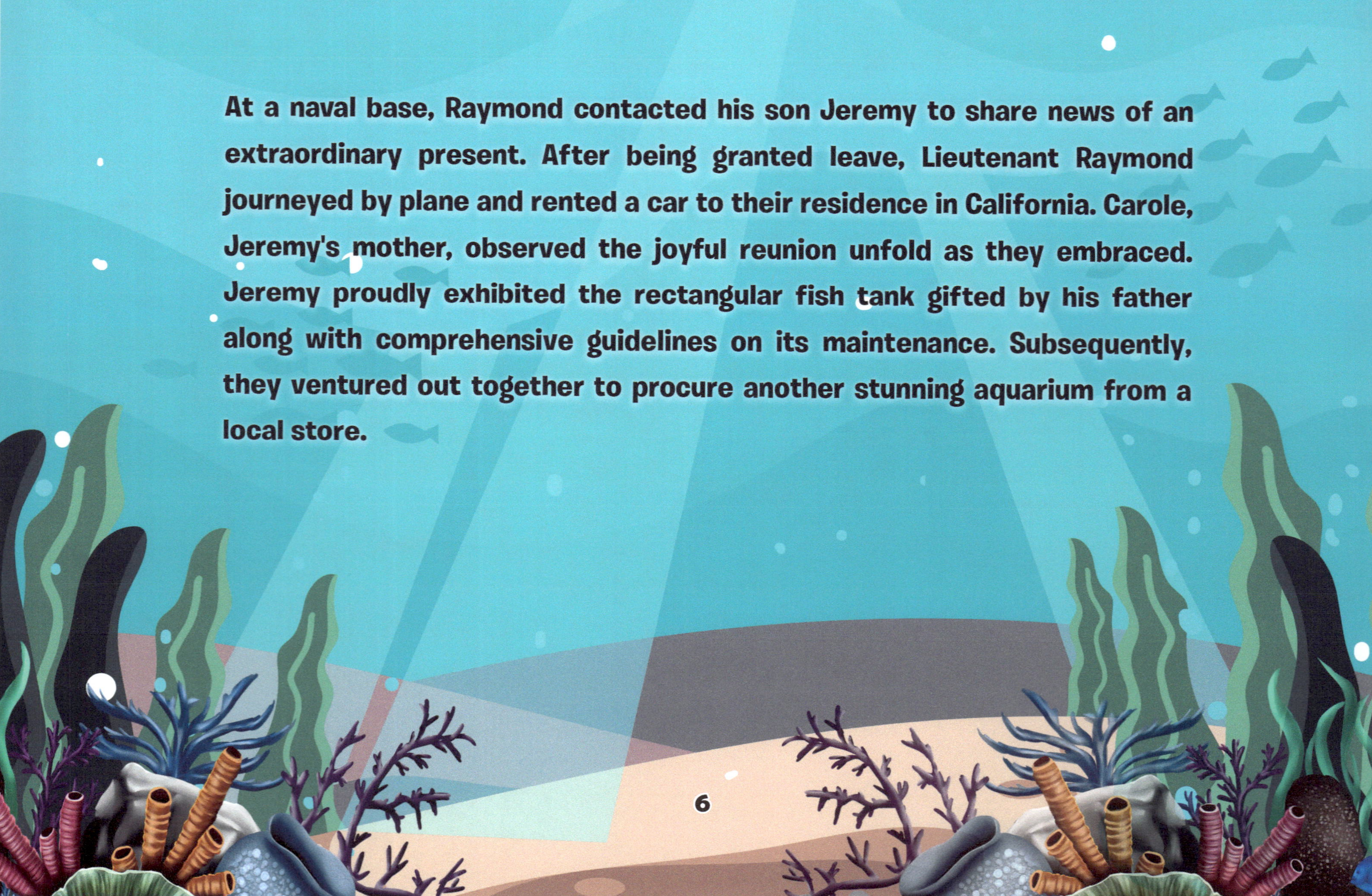

At a naval base, Raymond contacted his son Jeremy to share news of an extraordinary present. After being granted leave, Lieutenant Raymond journeyed by plane and rented a car to their residence in California. Carole, Jeremy's mother, observed the joyful reunion unfold as they embraced. Jeremy proudly exhibited the rectangular fish tank gifted by his father along with comprehensive guidelines on its maintenance. Subsequently, they ventured out together to procure another stunning aquarium from a local store.

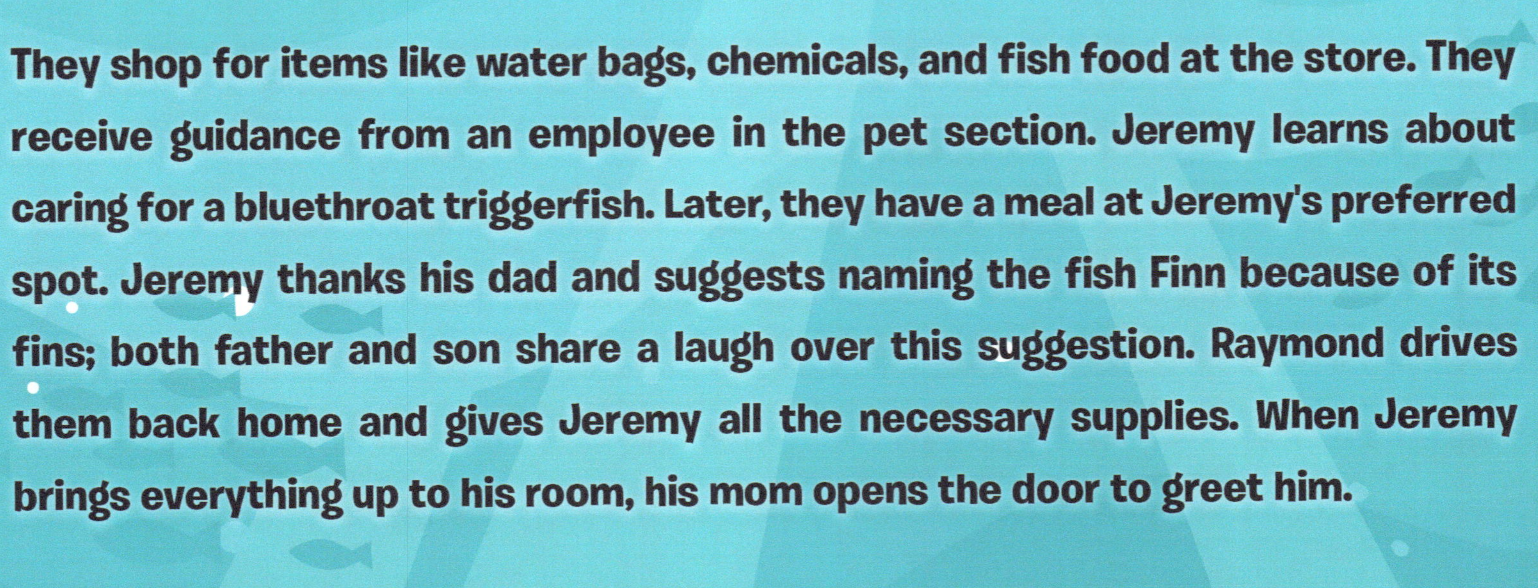

They shop for items like water bags, chemicals, and fish food at the store. They receive guidance from an employee in the pet section. Jeremy learns about caring for a bluethroat triggerfish. Later, they have a meal at Jeremy's preferred spot. Jeremy thanks his dad and suggests naming the fish Finn because of its fins; both father and son share a laugh over this suggestion. Raymond drives them back home and gives Jeremy all the necessary supplies. When Jeremy brings everything up to his room, his mom opens the door to greet him.

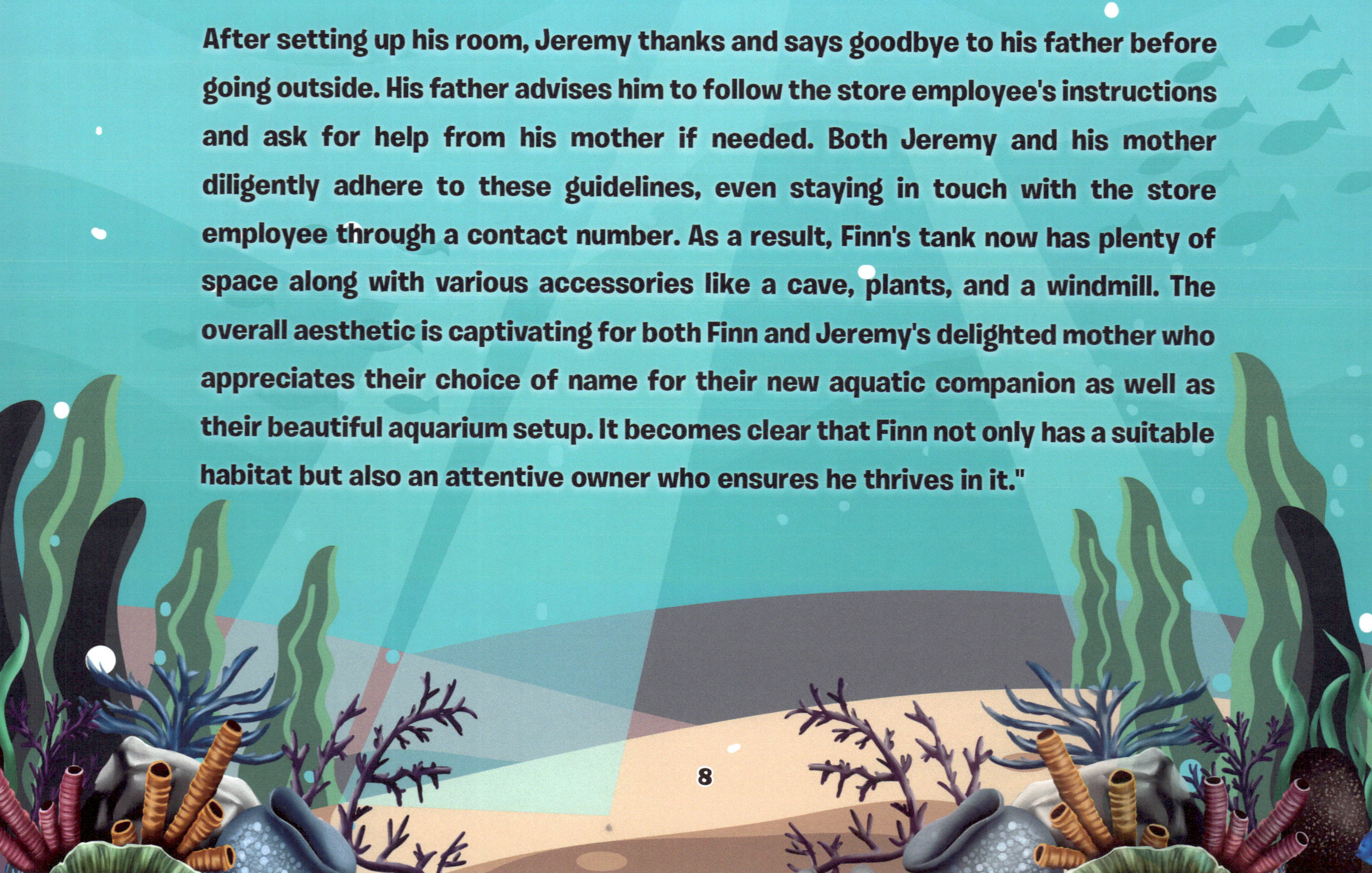

After setting up his room, Jeremy thanks and says goodbye to his father before going outside. His father advises him to follow the store employee's instructions and ask for help from his mother if needed. Both Jeremy and his mother diligently adhere to these guidelines, even staying in touch with the store employee through a contact number. As a result, Finn's tank now has plenty of space along with various accessories like a cave, plants, and a windmill. The overall aesthetic is captivating for both Finn and Jeremy's delighted mother who appreciates their choice of name for their new aquatic companion as well as their beautiful aquarium setup. It becomes clear that Finn not only has a suitable habitat but also an attentive owner who ensures he thrives in it."

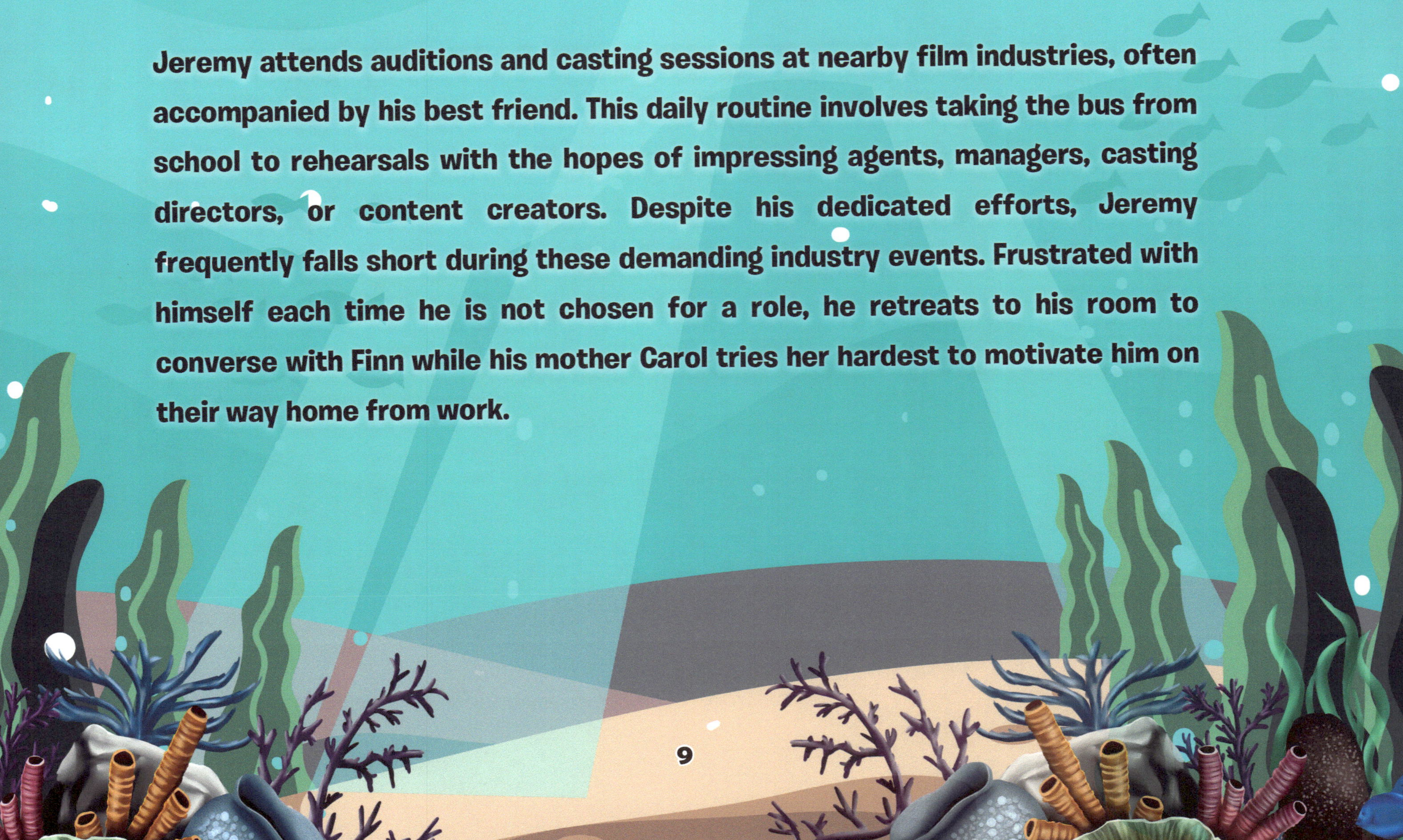

Jeremy attends auditions and casting sessions at nearby film industries, often accompanied by his best friend. This daily routine involves taking the bus from school to rehearsals with the hopes of impressing agents, managers, casting directors, or content creators. Despite his dedicated efforts, Jeremy frequently falls short during these demanding industry events. Frustrated with himself each time he is not chosen for a role, he retreats to his room to converse with Finn while his mother Carol tries her hardest to motivate him on their way home from work.

Carol is originally from Japan but was raised in California, where she encountered Raymond and they had a son together. Carol, having personal experience in the talent industry, possesses extensive knowledge about it and provides valuable advice to Jeremy. Despite their demanding careers that ultimately led to their separation, Carol and Raymond remain good friends. It is remarkable how closely connected Jeremy is with Finn; their bond resembles that of brothers. Finn communicates non-verbally by nodding his head sideways for negative responses and up and down for positive ones–an aspect unknown to most people around them. With school commitments alongside rehearsals, practices, auditions, and castings, Jeremy lives a rather hectic life. He keeps Finn's abilities secret from his friends as well as the true extent of Finn's exceptional qualities.

The origin of Finn is truly remarkable. According to its definition, Finn can be considered a magnificent work of magic that was once owned by an esteemed Samurai. The Samurai would retreat to a secluded area in Japan for deep meditation and tranquility. During one of these sessions, the great spiritual authority instructed the Samurai to carefully place a rare and precious blue triggerfish from the magical pond known as "the living pond" into a plastic bag along with water from it. Further instructions were given by the spiritual authority for placing this unique blue-throat triggerfish inside a specially designed cubic aquarium adorned with ancient writings and drawings that date back centuries.

The supreme spiritual entity instructed the esteemed samurai to present a unique offering to Japan's royal family. Bestowing this extraordinary honor, the royal family, in tune with their spiritual experiences, recognizes and accepts this exceedingly exceptional gift. Directly bestowed with profound spiritual insights by the higher authority, they are well aware of how crucial it is to safeguard this special gift at all costs. They possess intuitive knowledge of when and where precisely the blue throat triggerfish should be presented and comprehend its greater significance. Throughout the generations, the royal family lineage persists until Leah is born. In her exceptional era, Leah's encounter with a bluethroat triggerfish makes a strong impression on her. As she grows older, she recognizes the significance of this fish and believes it serves a special purpose. With conviction, Leah embraces the belief that an extraordinary event will occur in the future as a sign of things to come.

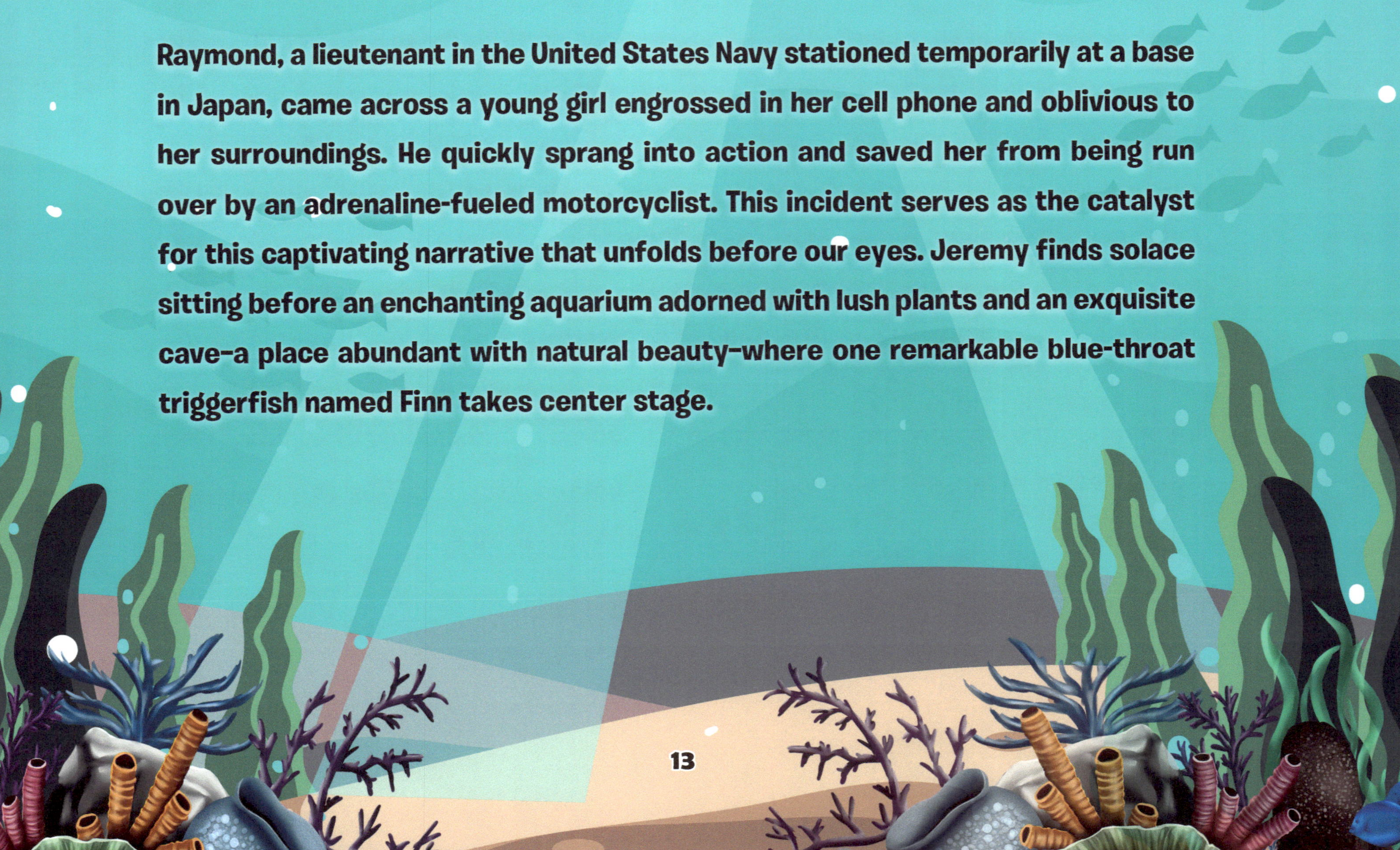

Raymond, a lieutenant in the United States Navy stationed temporarily at a base in Japan, came across a young girl engrossed in her cell phone and oblivious to her surroundings. He quickly sprang into action and saved her from being run over by an adrenaline-fueled motorcyclist. This incident serves as the catalyst for this captivating narrative that unfolds before our eyes. Jeremy finds solace sitting before an enchanting aquarium adorned with lush plants and an exquisite cave–a place abundant with natural beauty–where one remarkable blue-throat triggerfish named Finn takes center stage.

On a particular occasion, Jeremy's ongoing complaints and honest emotions towards Finn lead to an unexpected occurrence. Suddenly, an idea is planted in Jeremy's mind by Finn: he urges him to put his finger inside the aquarium and touch Finn. Without hesitation, Jeremy follows these instructions - reaching into the aquarium with one finger to make contact with Finn. In an astonishing turn of events, Jeremy finds himself shrinking down to the same size as Finn within the confines of the aquarium. Equipped with swimming shorts, goggles, and a peculiar apparatus in his mouth along with a waterproof watch that accurately displays time relative to their world - even indicating when Jeremy's mother will arrive home -Jeremy is overcome by shock and disbelief. However, Finn embraces him reassuringly while communicating clearly like in any ordinary conversation. He assures Jeremy that everything will be okay.

Finn assures Jeremy that he is a magical blue-throat triggerfish named 1313 and there's no need to worry. He explains that in this place, time passes much faster than in his world, but Jeremy can go back anytime he wants. Finn's existence is only known by the royal family and it's a secret. If Jeremy's mom comes knocking on his bedroom door, all he has to do is touch Finn again and he will instantly appear back in his room, completely dry. This transformation process is completely safe and it allows Finn to show him the magnificent underwater kingdom.

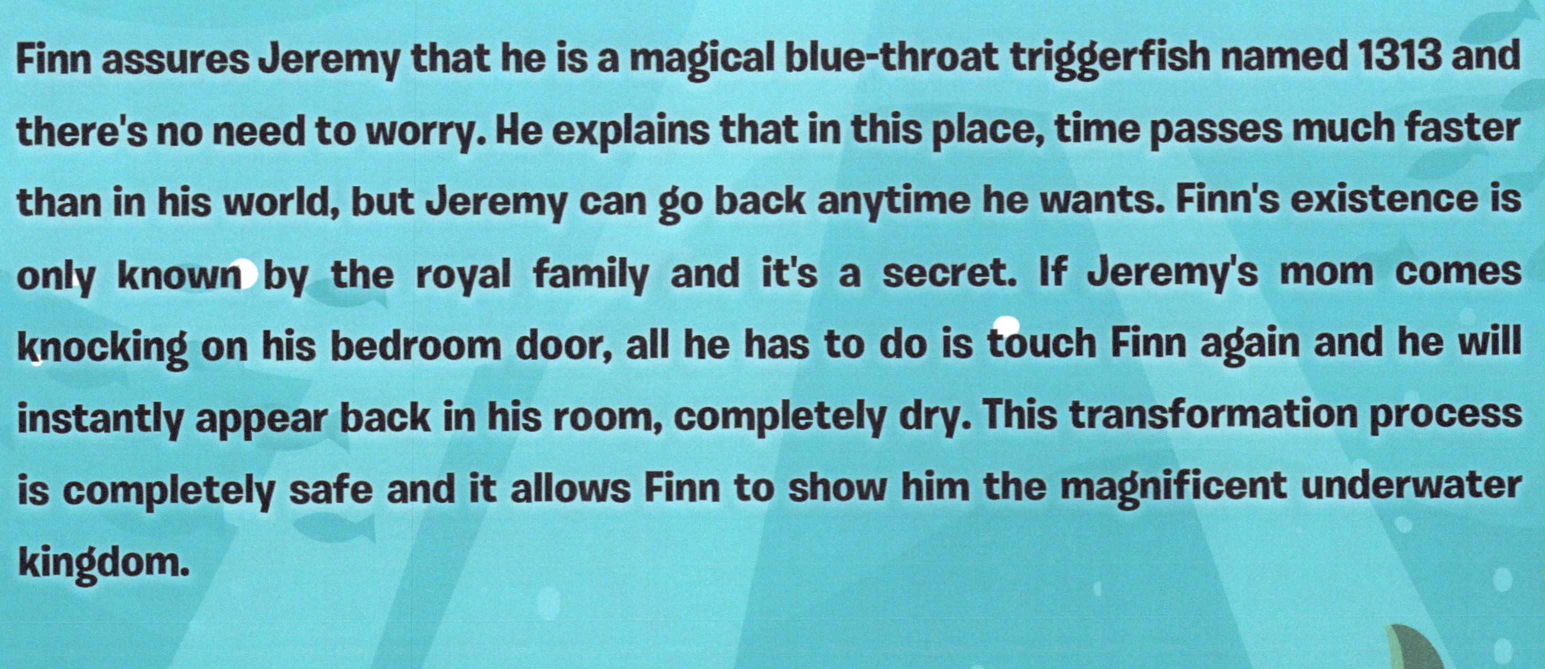

Jeremy is in awe as Finn describes an incredible underwater kingdom filled with majestic beauty. Finn mentions the mesmerizing Broadway shows performed by hundreds of diverse underwater species, showcasing the most captivating displays ever witnessed. Among them, there is even an astonishing octopus symphony orchestra performing their own enchanting compositions.

THE OCTOPUS UNDERWATER SYMPHONY ORCHESTRA
17

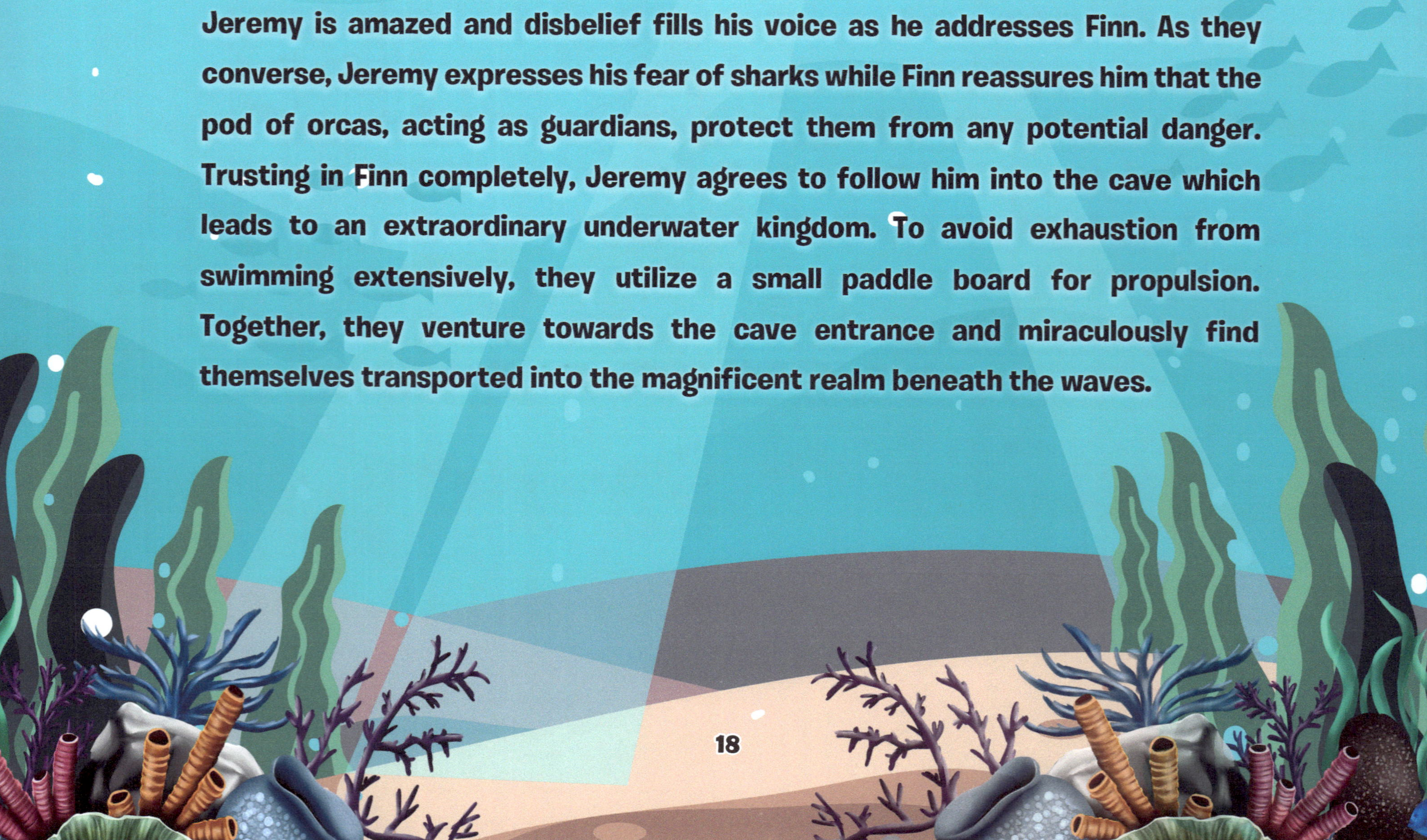

Jeremy is amazed and disbelief fills his voice as he addresses Finn. As they converse, Jeremy expresses his fear of sharks while Finn reassures him that the pod of orcas, acting as guardians, protect them from any potential danger. Trusting in Finn completely, Jeremy agrees to follow him into the cave which leads to an extraordinary underwater kingdom. To avoid exhaustion from swimming extensively, they utilize a small paddle board for propulsion. Together, they venture towards the cave entrance and miraculously find themselves transported into the magnificent realm beneath the waves.

Jeremy is in awe, unable to believe what he's witnessing. Finn, on the other hand, finds it absolutely beautiful. As they approach the auditorium, a spectacular sight unfolds before them: hundreds of schools of fish gathered inside an enormous seashell that spans over one hundred feet in length and width. The guardians stand tall, providing impressive security as ushers warmly greet guests. Jeremy can't help but notice the kelp transformed into rollercoaster tracks for seashell trains pulled by graceful seahorses - all designed for entertaining baby fishes. Completely speechless, Jeremy whispers to Finn about how unreal this entire underwater kingdom feels to him. Finn assures him that meeting his friends and experiencing the breathtaking underwater shows will be even more astonishing.

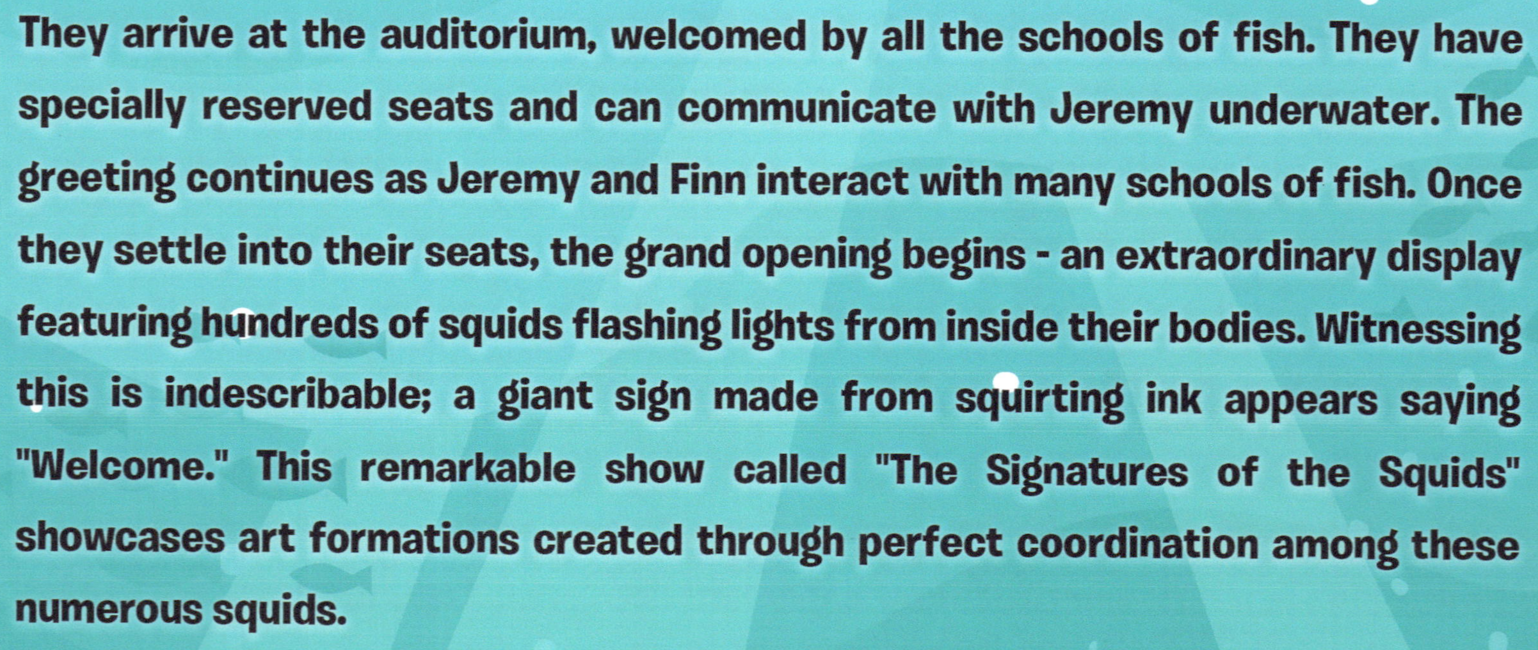

They arrive at the auditorium, welcomed by all the schools of fish. They have specially reserved seats and can communicate with Jeremy underwater. The greeting continues as Jeremy and Finn interact with many schools of fish. Once they settle into their seats, the grand opening begins - an extraordinary display featuring hundreds of squids flashing lights from inside their bodies. Witnessing this is indescribable; a giant sign made from squirting ink appears saying "Welcome." This remarkable show called "The Signatures of the Squids" showcases art formations created through perfect coordination among these numerous squids.

SIGNATURE OF THE SQUIDS

The grand opening displays include a captivating underwater symphony orchestra featuring schools of octopuses led by an incredible music conductor. This remarkable orchestra consists of forty highly skilled octopuses, each showcasing extraordinary talents. They perform flawlessly in perfect coordination, delivering a breathtaking musical show. The ushers for each performance are penguins. Following this is the ballet of the stingrays, with hundreds appearing in flawless formations.

BALLET OF STINGRAYS

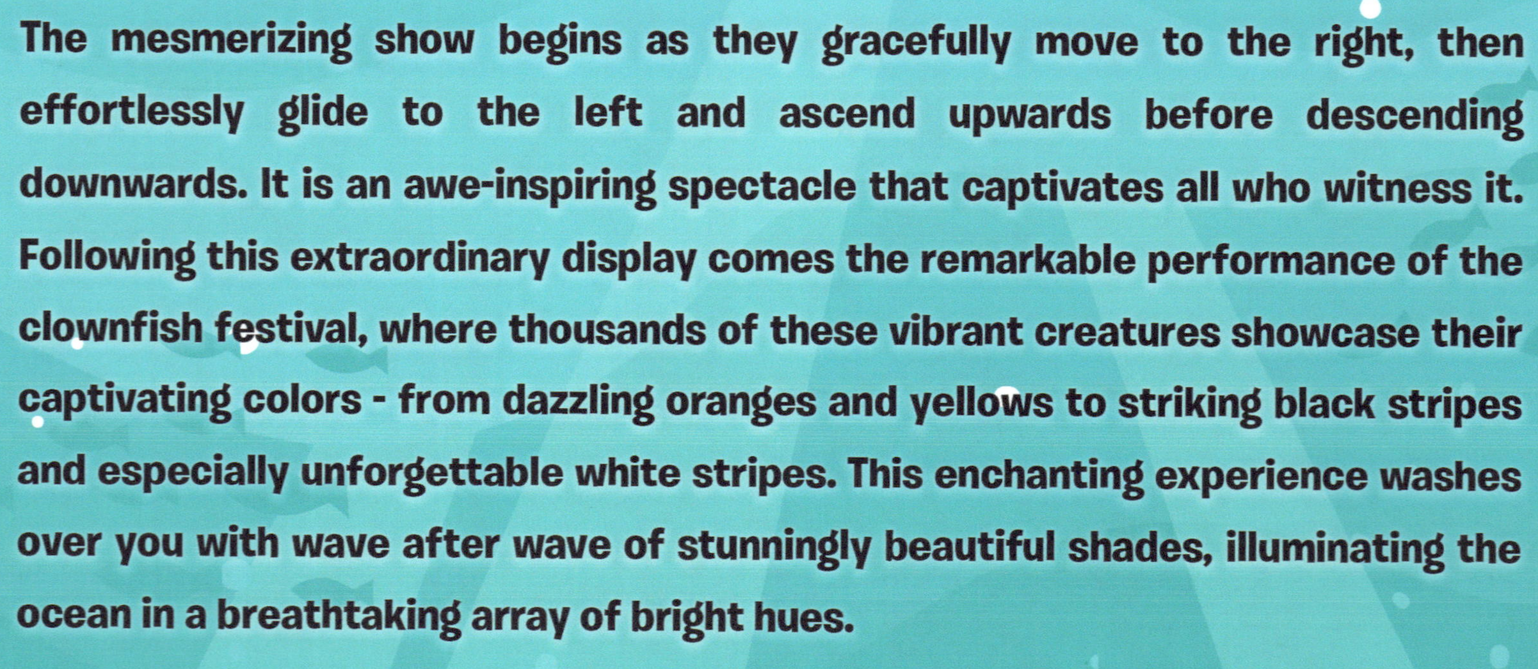

The mesmerizing show begins as they gracefully move to the right, then effortlessly glide to the left and ascend upwards before descending downwards. It is an awe-inspiring spectacle that captivates all who witness it. Following this extraordinary display comes the remarkable performance of the clownfish festival, where thousands of these vibrant creatures showcase their captivating colors - from dazzling oranges and yellows to striking black stripes and especially unforgettable white stripes. This enchanting experience washes over you with wave after wave of stunningly beautiful shades, illuminating the ocean in a breathtaking array of bright hues.

CLOWNFISH FESTIVAL

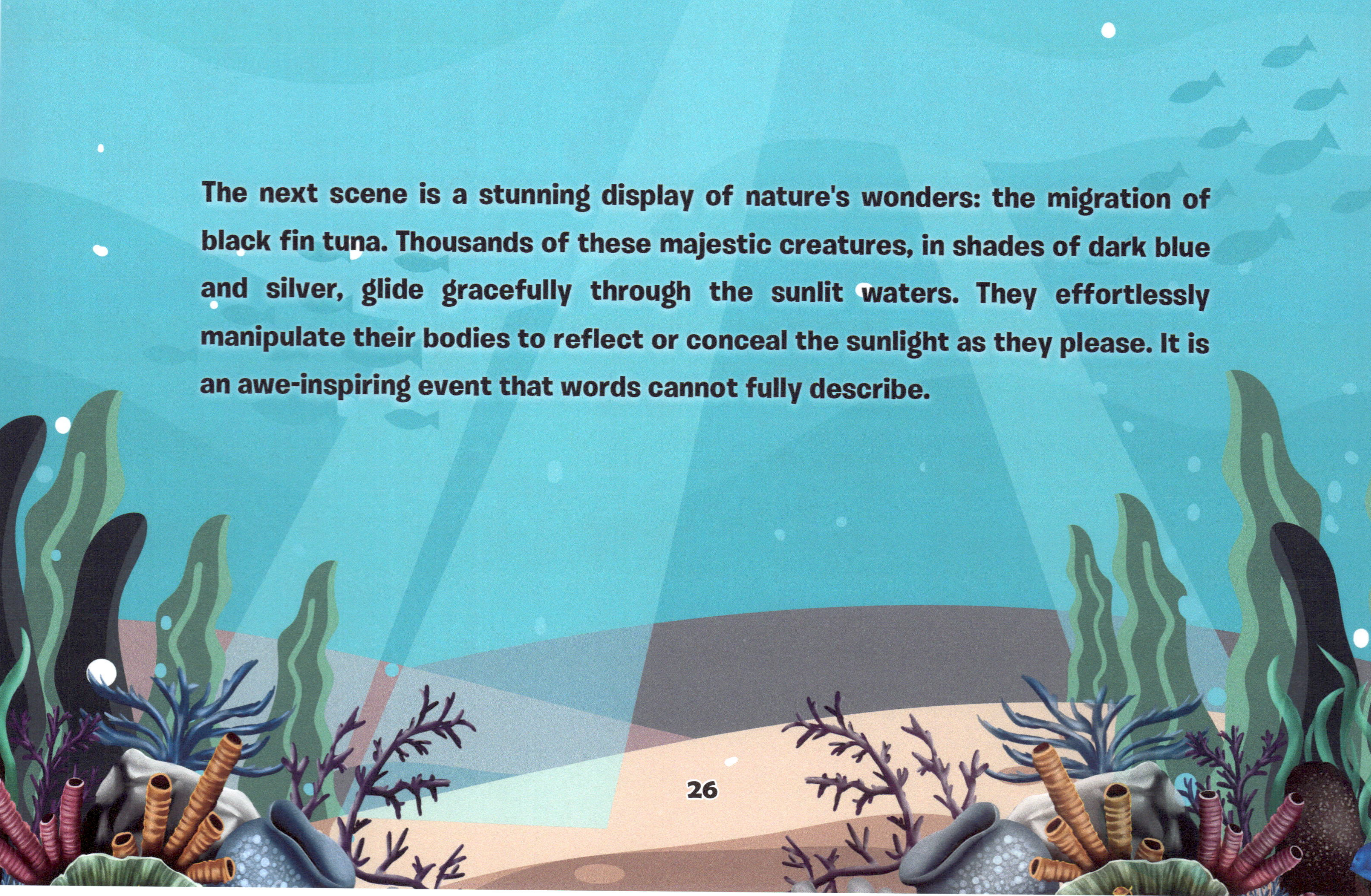

The next scene is a stunning display of nature's wonders: the migration of black fin tuna. Thousands of these majestic creatures, in shades of dark blue and silver, glide gracefully through the sunlit waters. They effortlessly manipulate their bodies to reflect or conceal the sunlight as they please. It is an awe-inspiring event that words cannot fully describe.

TUNA HEAVEN
27

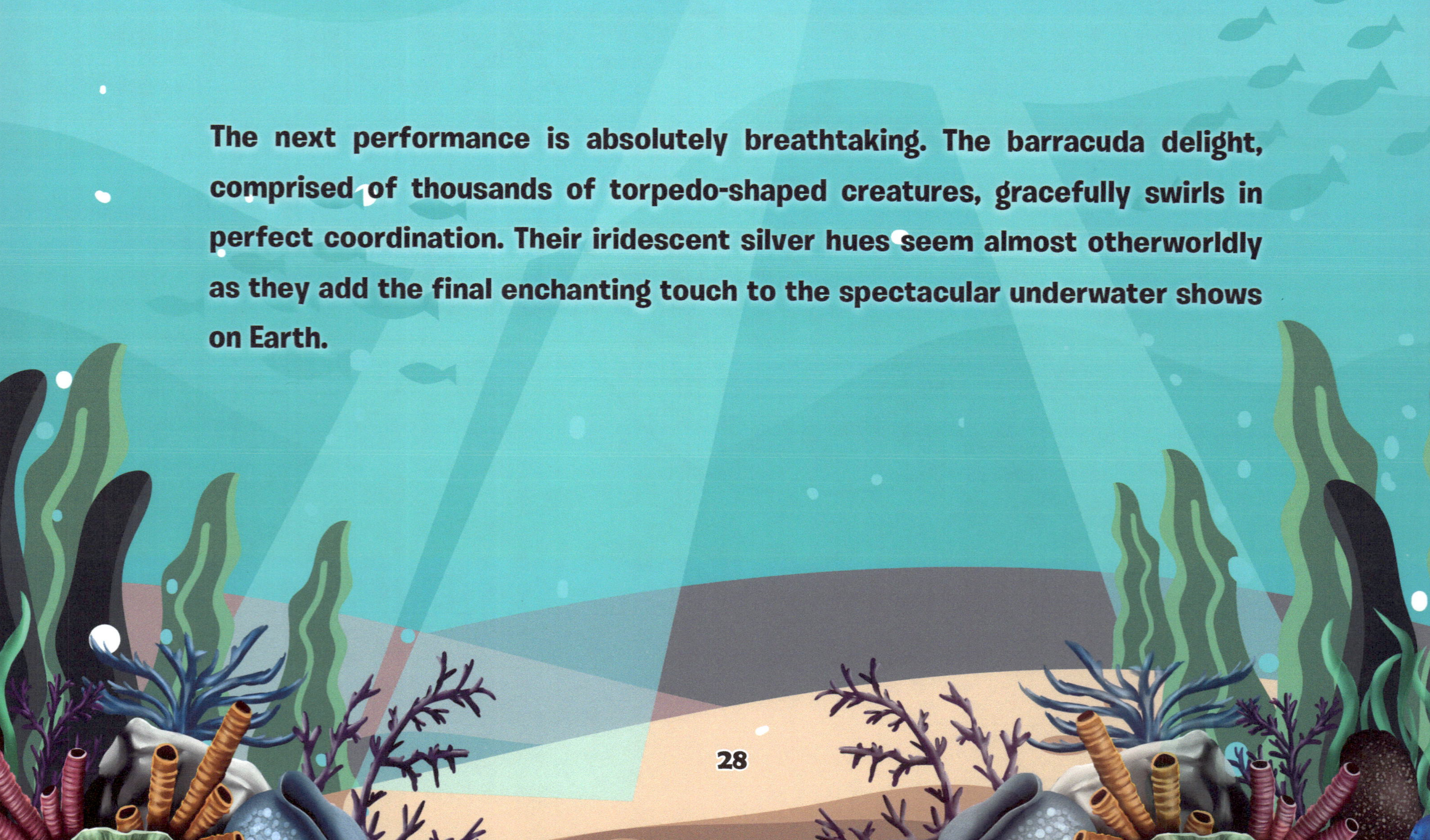

The next performance is absolutely breathtaking. The barracuda delight, comprised of thousands of torpedo-shaped creatures, gracefully swirls in perfect coordination. Their iridescent silver hues seem almost otherworldly as they add the final enchanting touch to the spectacular underwater shows on Earth.

BARRACUDA DELIGHT

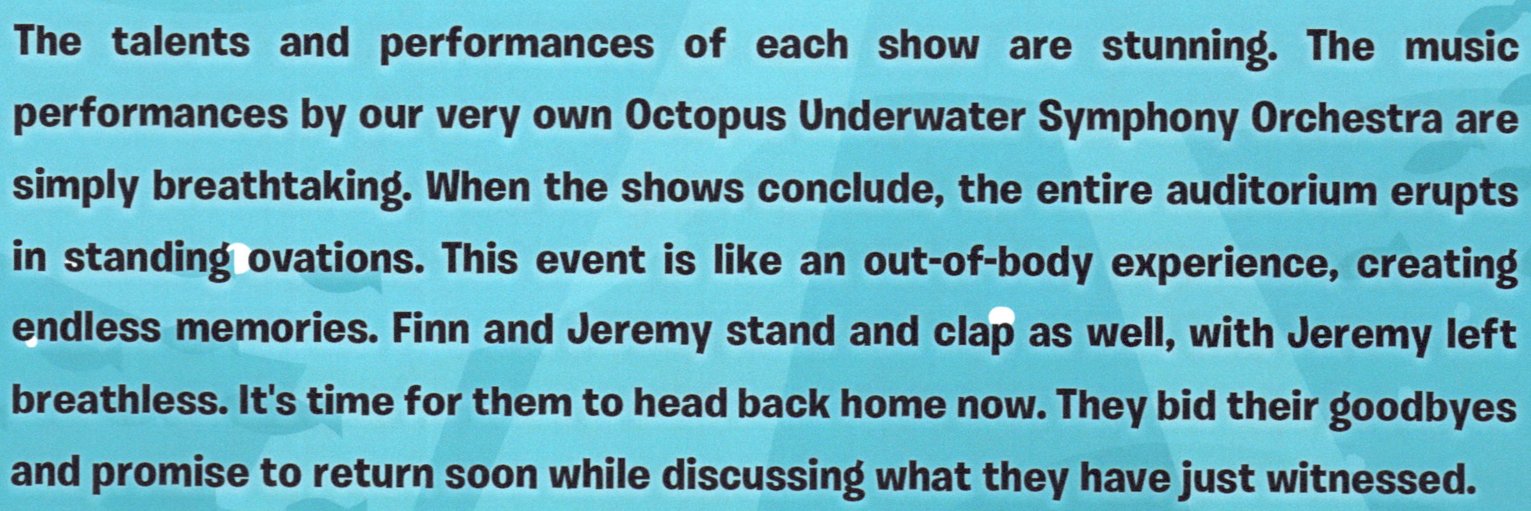

The talents and performances of each show are stunning. The music performances by our very own Octopus Underwater Symphony Orchestra are simply breathtaking. When the shows conclude, the entire auditorium erupts in standing ovations. This event is like an out-of-body experience, creating endless memories. Finn and Jeremy stand and clap as well, with Jeremy left breathless. It's time for them to head back home now. They bid their goodbyes and promise to return soon while discussing what they have just witnessed.

Finn tells Jeremy, "I've always believed that time seems to pass more quickly in the magical underwater kingdom." Jeremy responds, "I have never witnessed anything so mesmerizing. The shows, exhibits, music, and vibrant visuals are beyond words." With a playful smile, Finn asks Jeremy if he thinks all of this will enhance his auditions and casting opportunities. Jeremy confidently states that it has ignited a new level of artistic prowess within him.

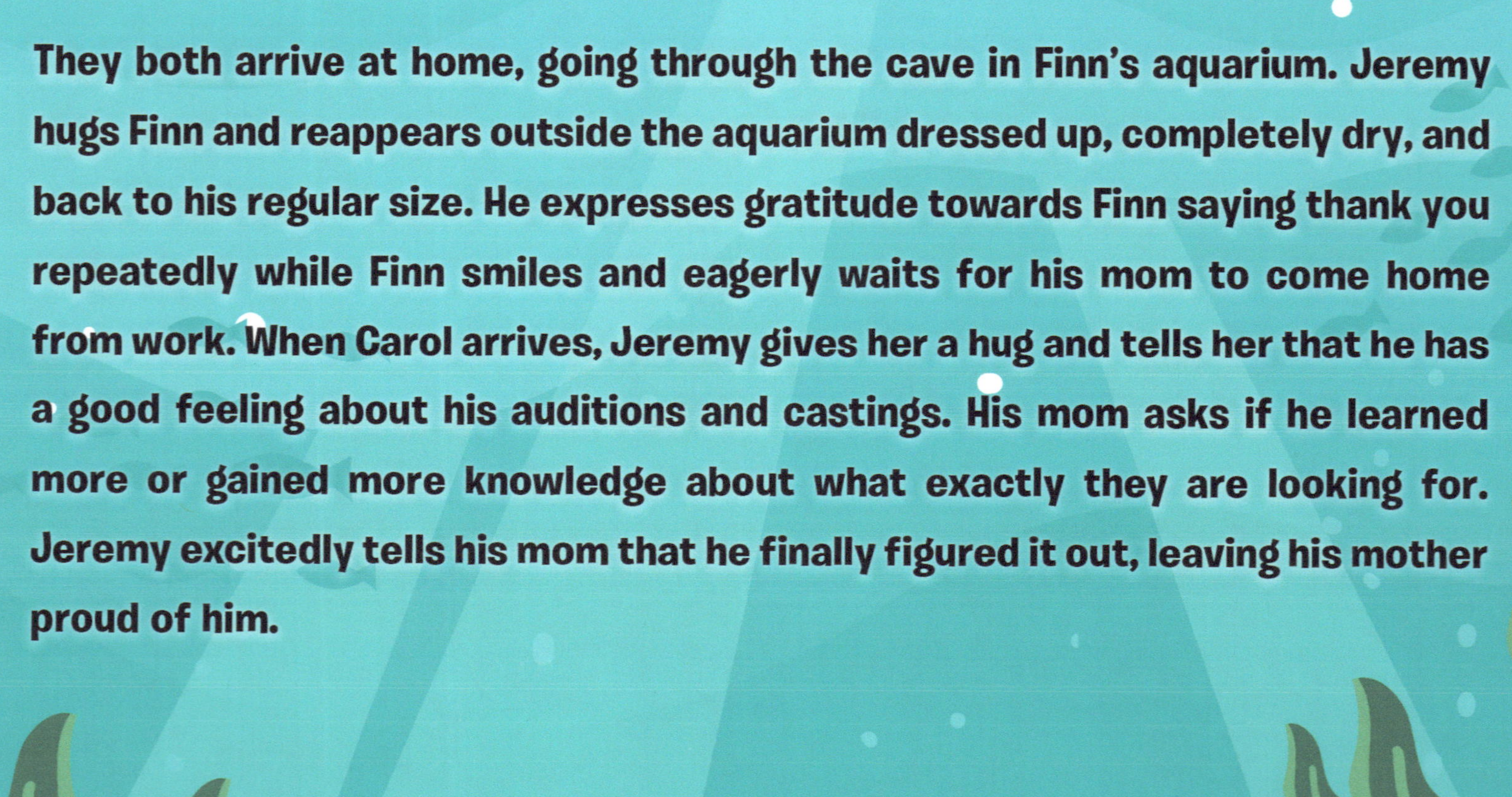

They both arrive at home, going through the cave in Finn's aquarium. Jeremy hugs Finn and reappears outside the aquarium dressed up, completely dry, and back to his regular size. He expresses gratitude towards Finn saying thank you repeatedly while Finn smiles and eagerly waits for his mom to come home from work. When Carol arrives, Jeremy gives her a hug and tells her that he has a good feeling about his auditions and castings. His mom asks if he learned more or gained more knowledge about what exactly they are looking for. Jeremy excitedly tells his mom that he finally figured it out, leaving his mother proud of him.

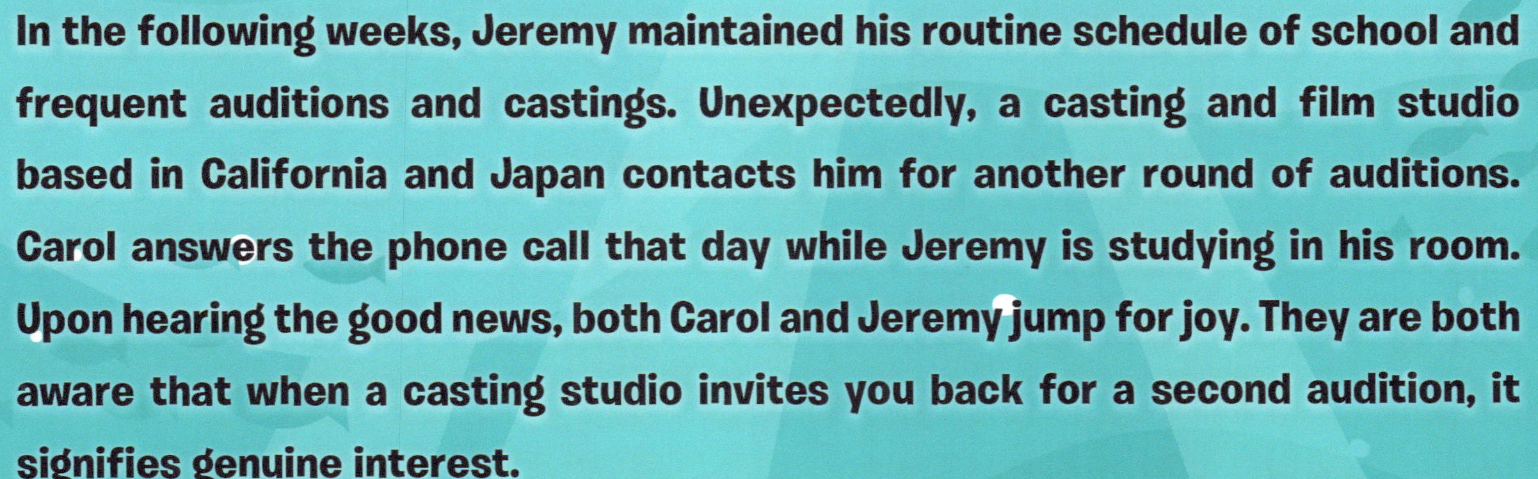

In the following weeks, Jeremy maintained his routine schedule of school and frequent auditions and castings. Unexpectedly, a casting and film studio based in California and Japan contacts him for another round of auditions. Carol answers the phone call that day while Jeremy is studying in his room. Upon hearing the good news, both Carol and Jeremy jump for joy. They are both aware that when a casting studio invites you back for a second audition, it signifies genuine interest.

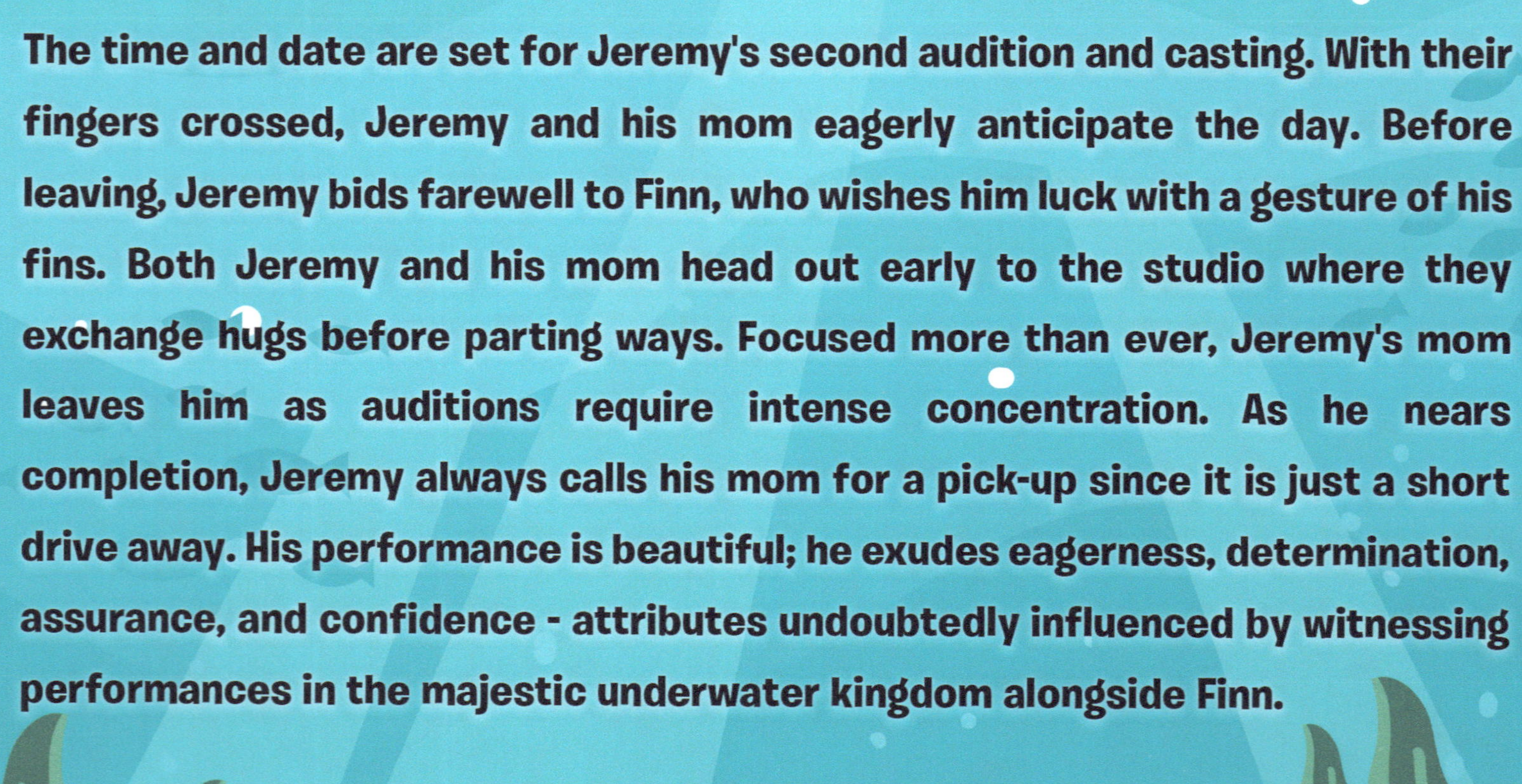

The time and date are set for Jeremy's second audition and casting. With their fingers crossed, Jeremy and his mom eagerly anticipate the day. Before leaving, Jeremy bids farewell to Finn, who wishes him luck with a gesture of his fins. Both Jeremy and his mom head out early to the studio where they exchange hugs before parting ways. Focused more than ever, Jeremy's mom leaves him as auditions require intense concentration. As he nears completion, Jeremy always calls his mom for a pick-up since it is just a short drive away. His performance is beautiful; he exudes eagerness, determination, assurance, and confidence - attributes undoubtedly influenced by witnessing performances in the majestic underwater kingdom alongside Finn.

Jeremy was selected by the casting and film studio for a Broadway-style show. The initial performance will be in Japan, with all expenses covered by the studio. These events are scheduled to align with Jeremy's school breaks and his mother's days off from work. Planning everything in advance ensures that no stress is placed on families, and word of this exciting opportunity spreads quickly.

In just a couple of weeks, the show will take place in Japan. Jeremy excitedly shares the news with his dad, Finn. When his dad receives the news, he is overjoyed. Even Jeremy's fellow officers will attend the show due to special permission from the United States Navy. In addition, the royal family plans to be present at this extraordinary event along with their daughter Leah. The news spreads quickly and both Jeremy and his mom are astounded by the fact that even the royal family will be attending such an incredible show.

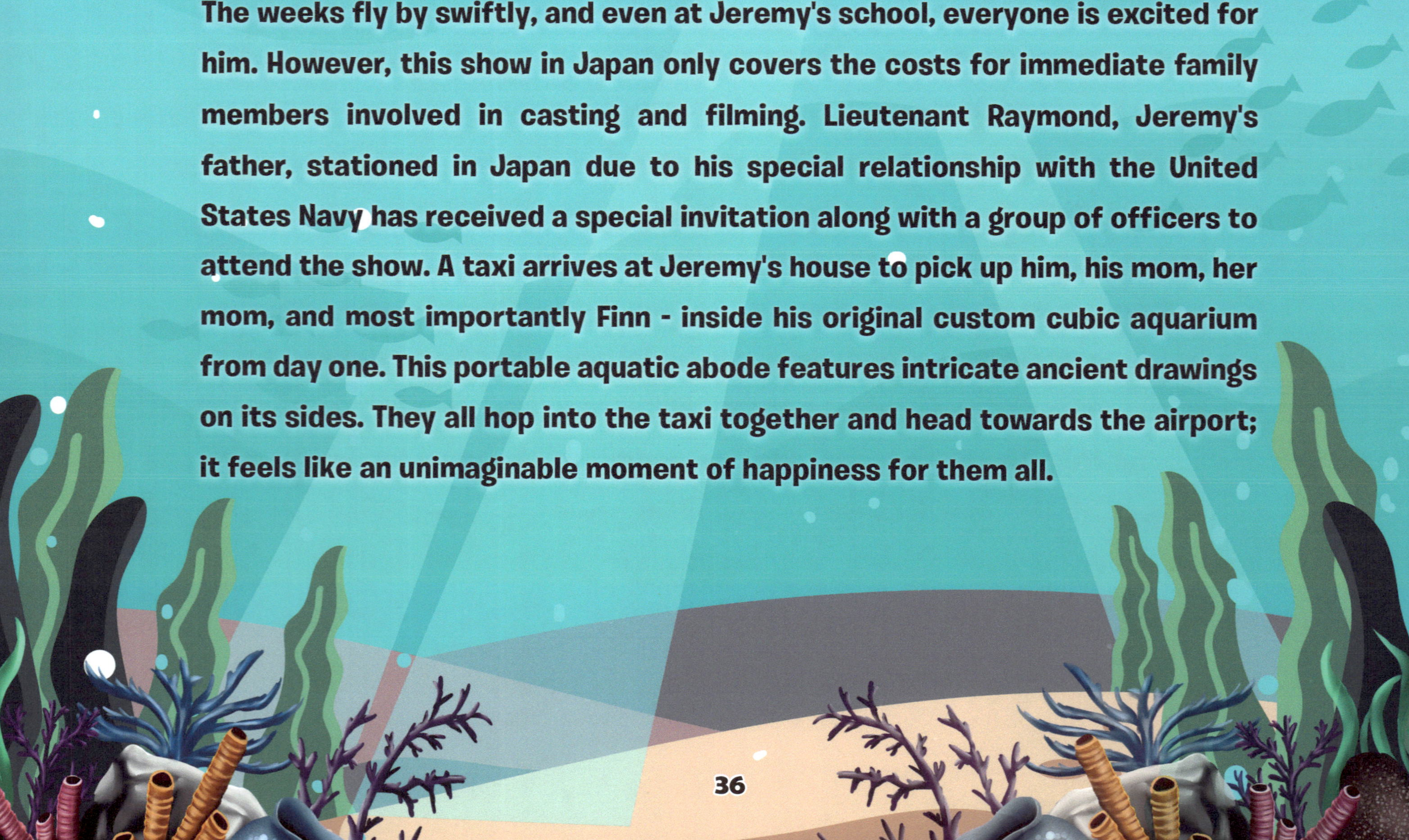

The weeks fly by swiftly, and even at Jeremy's school, everyone is excited for him. However, this show in Japan only covers the costs for immediate family members involved in casting and filming. Lieutenant Raymond, Jeremy's father, stationed in Japan due to his special relationship with the United States Navy has received a special invitation along with a group of officers to attend the show. A taxi arrives at Jeremy's house to pick up him, his mom, her mom, and most importantly Finn - inside his original custom cubic aquarium from day one. This portable aquatic abode features intricate ancient drawings on its sides. They all hop into the taxi together and head towards the airport; it feels like an unimaginable moment of happiness for them all.

Upon their arrival at the airport, they proceed to the terminal and await boarding. The casting and film studio attend to all their necessary arrangements. Once on board, they enjoy a pleasant flight, complete with various amenities such as food, refreshments, and video games. After many hours in transit, they finally reach Japan where a taxi driver holds up a sign bearing their family name for easy identification. They climb into the taxi and marvel at the breathtaking scenery along the way–the stunning architecture and rich cultural heritage of the country leave them in awe. Their hotel is equally remarkable when they arrive; after disembarking from the vehicle, they are informed by the driver that the pick-up time for rehearsals is 6:00 pm sharp. Taking some time to settle in and explore its grounds upon arrival before enjoying dinner within its premises prepares them well for an eventful evening ahead–awaiting transportation once again via taxi service.

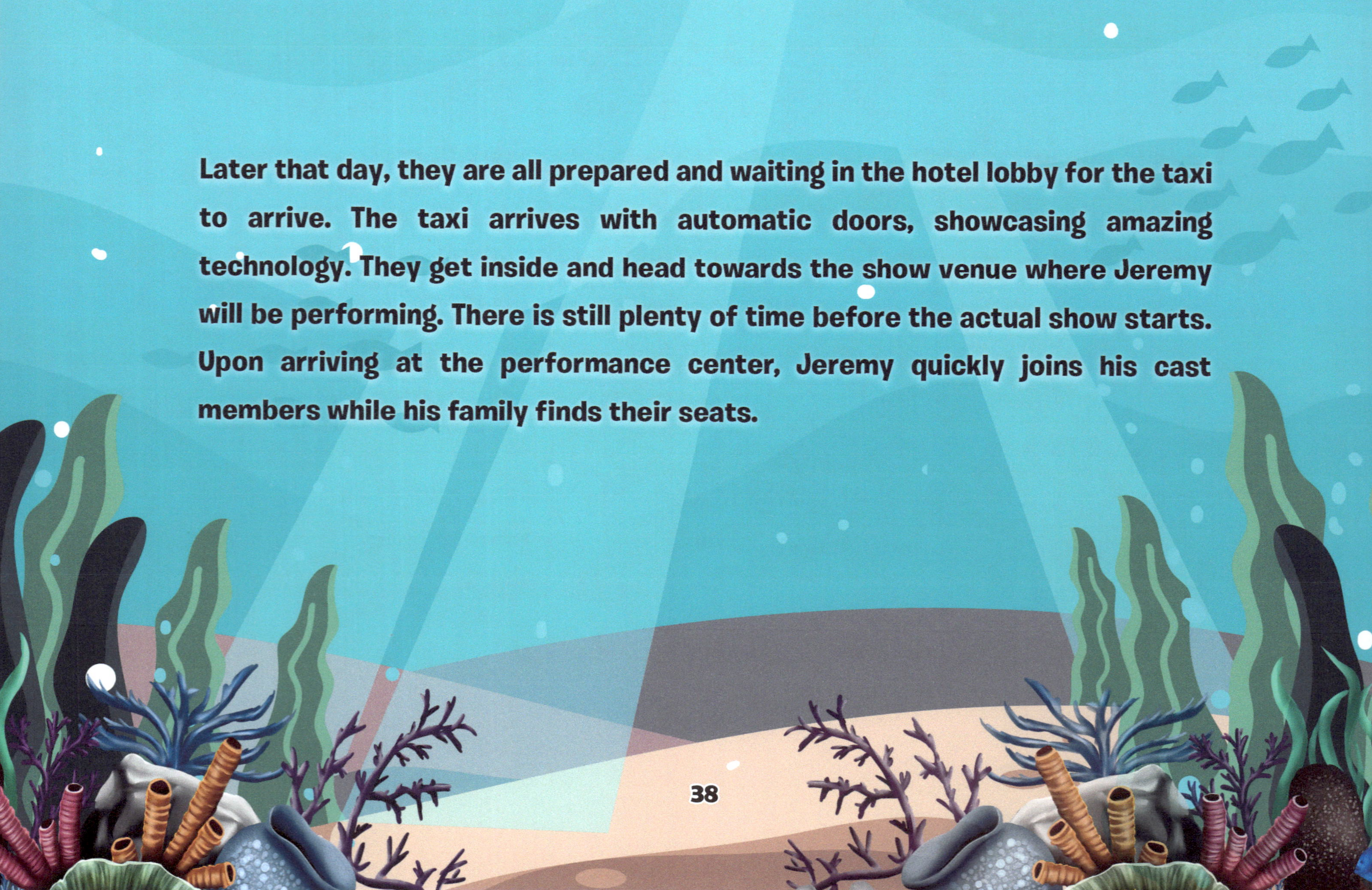

Later that day, they are all prepared and waiting in the hotel lobby for the taxi to arrive. The taxi arrives with automatic doors, showcasing amazing technology. They get inside and head towards the show venue where Jeremy will be performing. There is still plenty of time before the actual show starts. Upon arriving at the performance center, Jeremy quickly joins his cast members while his family finds their seats.

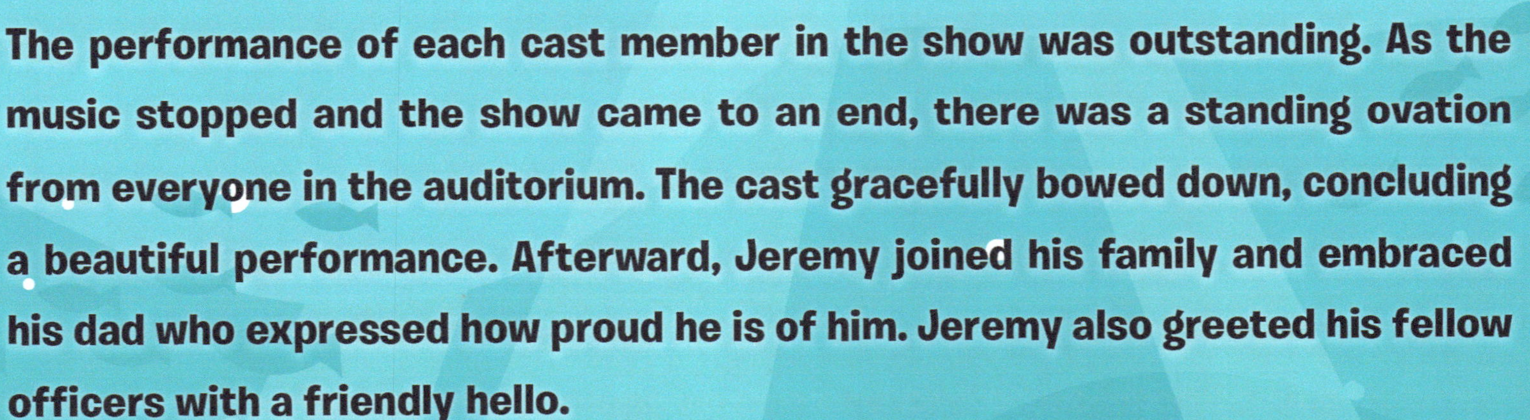

The performance of each cast member in the show was outstanding. As the music stopped and the show came to an end, there was a standing ovation from everyone in the auditorium. The cast gracefully bowed down, concluding a beautiful performance. Afterward, Jeremy joined his family and embraced his dad who expressed how proud he is of him. Jeremy also greeted his fellow officers with a friendly hello.

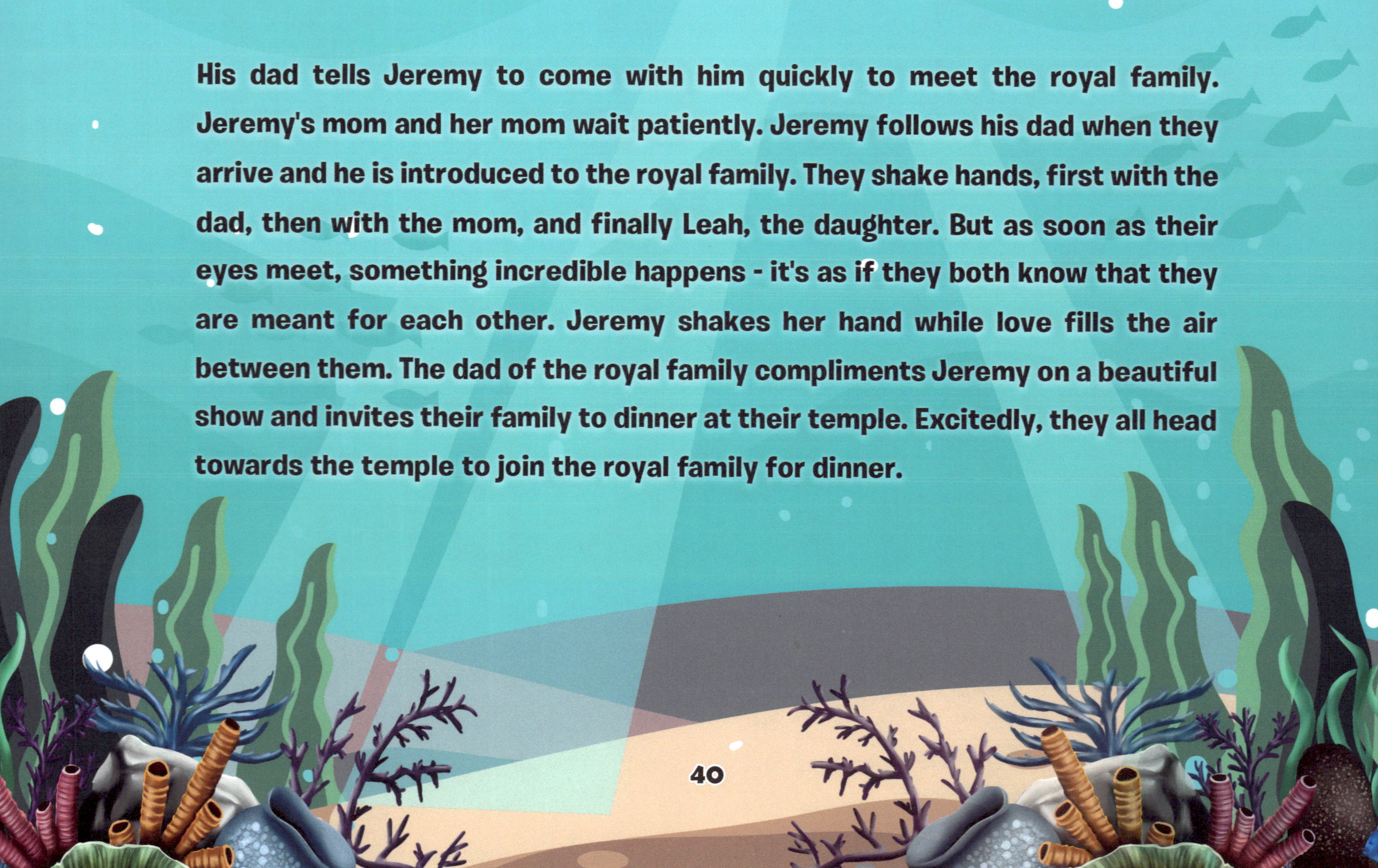

His dad tells Jeremy to come with him quickly to meet the royal family. Jeremy's mom and her mom wait patiently. Jeremy follows his dad when they arrive and he is introduced to the royal family. They shake hands, first with the dad, then with the mom, and finally Leah, the daughter. But as soon as their eyes meet, something incredible happens - it's as if they both know that they are meant for each other. Jeremy shakes her hand while love fills the air between them. The dad of the royal family compliments Jeremy on a beautiful show and invites their family to dinner at their temple. Excitedly, they all head towards the temple to join the royal family for dinner.

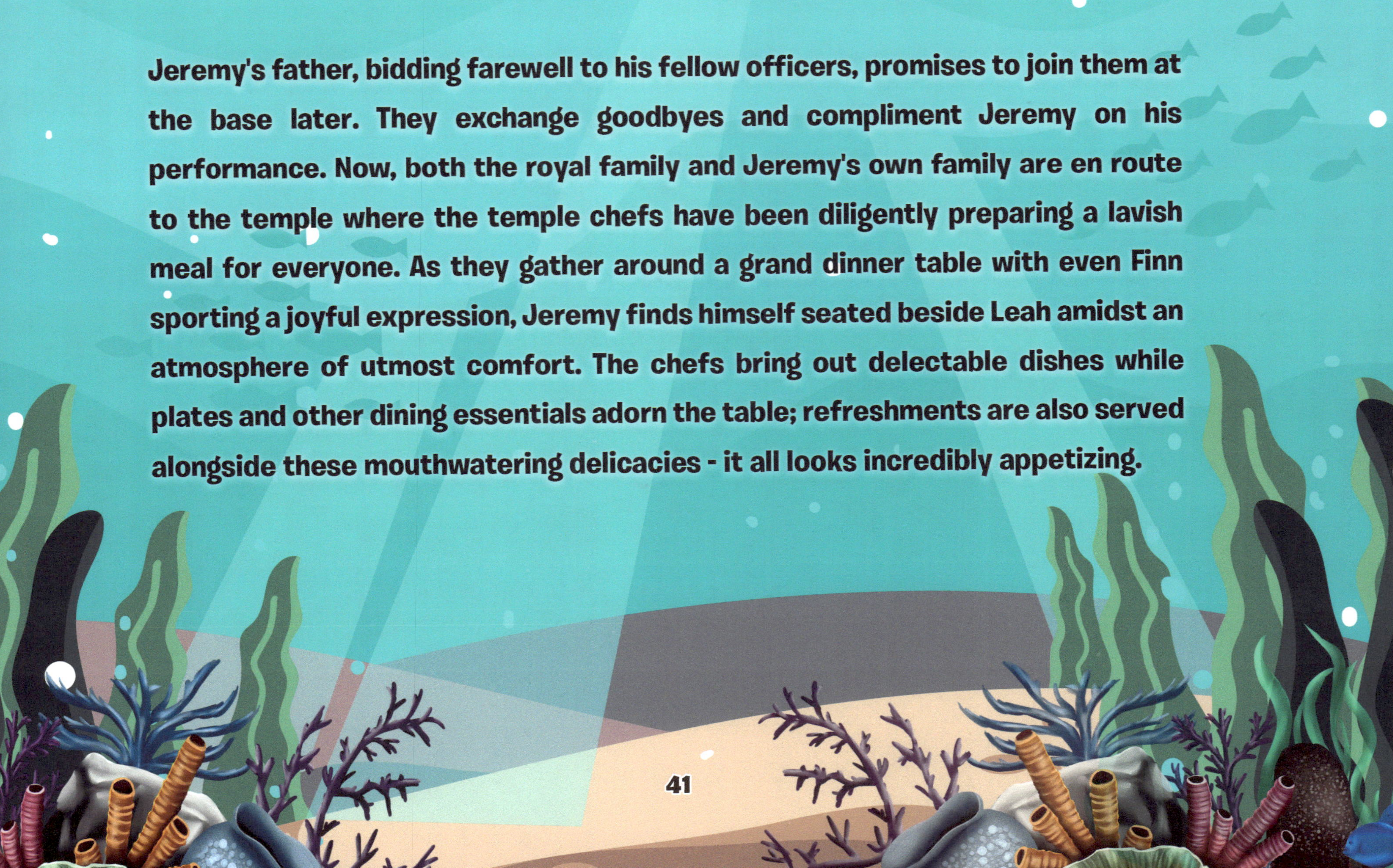

Jeremy's father, bidding farewell to his fellow officers, promises to join them at the base later. They exchange goodbyes and compliment Jeremy on his performance. Now, both the royal family and Jeremy's own family are en route to the temple where the temple chefs have been diligently preparing a lavish meal for everyone. As they gather around a grand dinner table with even Finn sporting a joyful expression, Jeremy finds himself seated beside Leah amidst an atmosphere of utmost comfort. The chefs bring out delectable dishes while plates and other dining essentials adorn the table; refreshments are also served alongside these mouthwatering delicacies - it all looks incredibly appetizing.

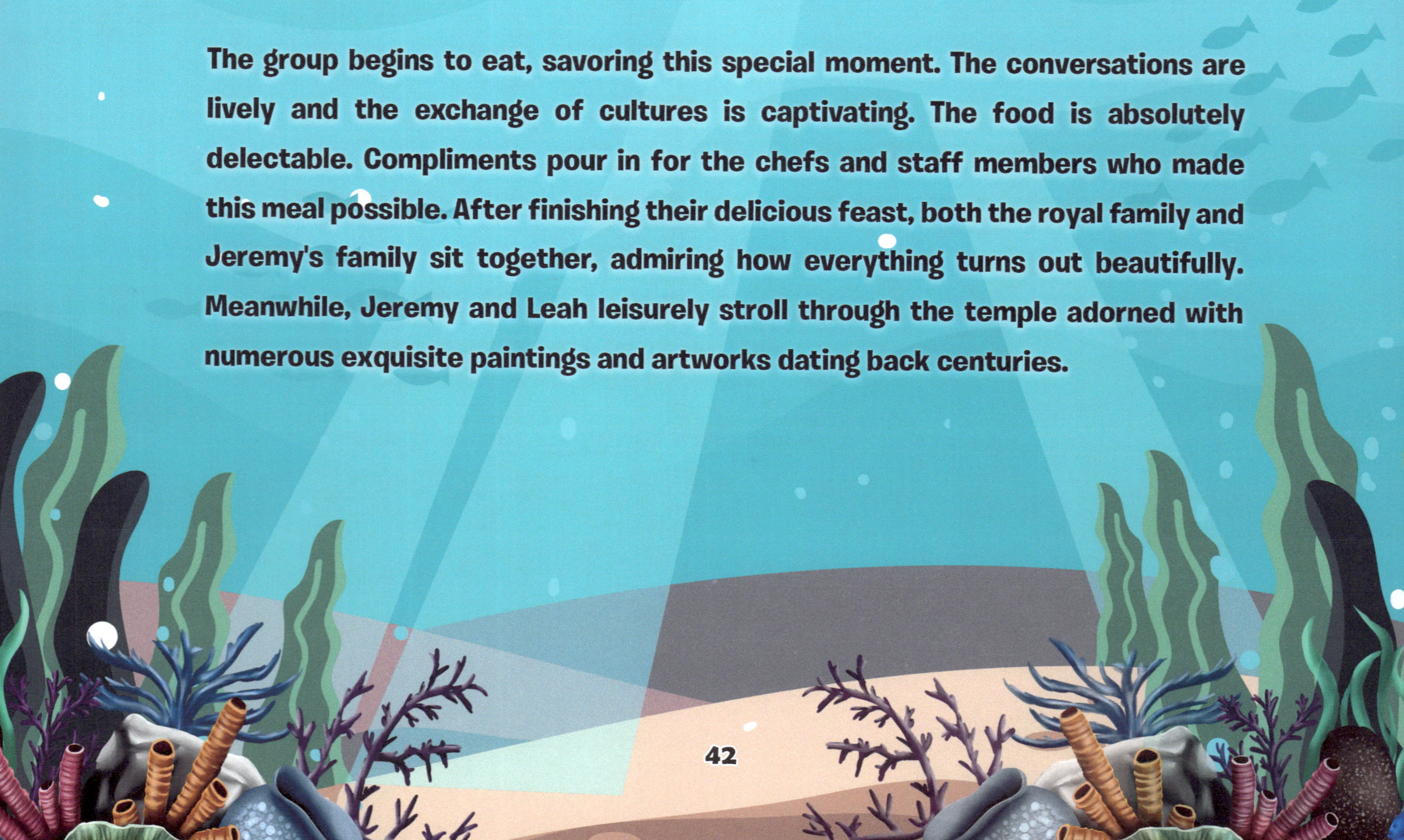

The group begins to eat, savoring this special moment. The conversations are lively and the exchange of cultures is captivating. The food is absolutely delectable. Compliments pour in for the chefs and staff members who made this meal possible. After finishing their delicious feast, both the royal family and Jeremy's family sit together, admiring how everything turns out beautifully. Meanwhile, Jeremy and Leah leisurely stroll through the temple adorned with numerous exquisite paintings and artworks dating back centuries.

The royal family has immense trust in Leah, recognizing her intelligence and the fact that she confides in them. Their familial bond is strong. While walking together, Jeremy expresses to Leah that she is the most beautiful girl he has ever seen, eliciting a smile from her. Deep down, they both feel destined for each other and make plans to maintain their close friendship - continuing conversations and spending time together. Over time, as Jeremy's family travels to Japan for his performances or when he performs in California, the royal family shows up to support him. The magnetic attraction between Jeremy and Leah only grows stronger; they are finishing high school with incredible aspirations while deeply loving each other. They remain constantly engaged in conversation with one another while finding solace in the knowledge that their families fully recognize their love and provide unwavering support.

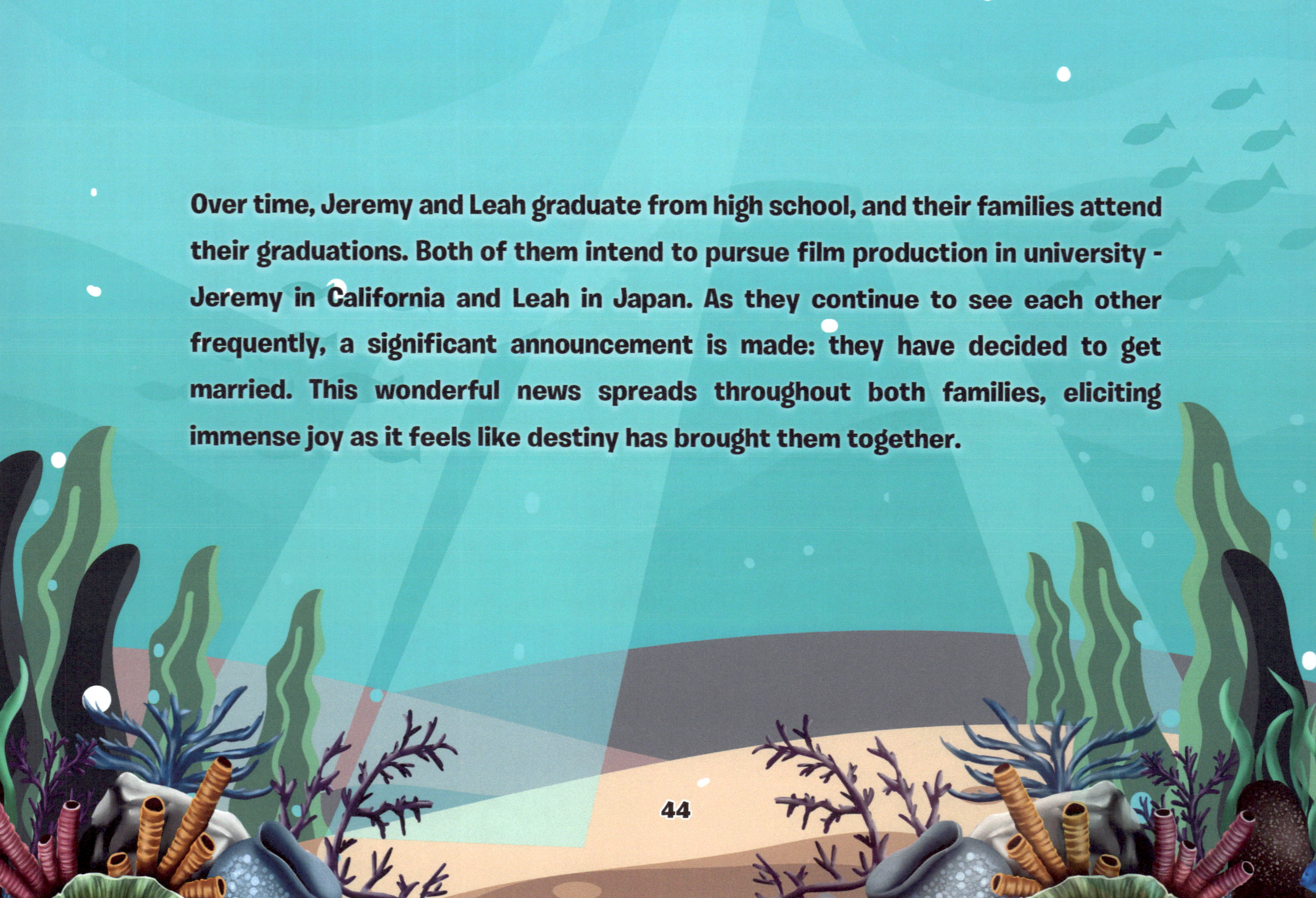

Over time, Jeremy and Leah graduate from high school, and their families attend their graduations. Both of them intend to pursue film production in university - Jeremy in California and Leah in Japan. As they continue to see each other frequently, a significant announcement is made: they have decided to get married. This wonderful news spreads throughout both families, eliciting immense joy as it feels like destiny has brought them together.

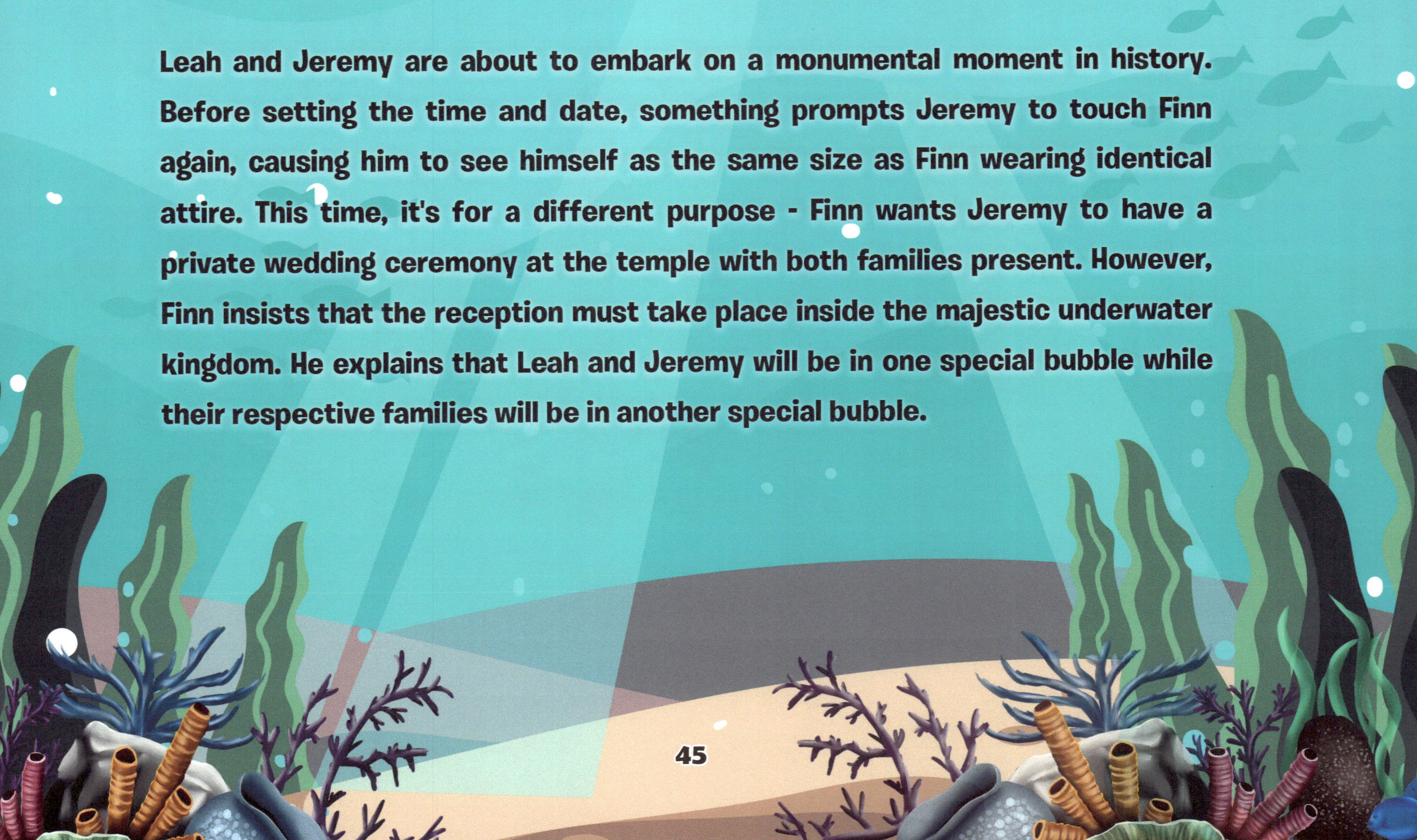

Leah and Jeremy are about to embark on a monumental moment in history. Before setting the time and date, something prompts Jeremy to touch Finn again, causing him to see himself as the same size as Finn wearing identical attire. This time, it's for a different purpose - Finn wants Jeremy to have a private wedding ceremony at the temple with both families present. However, Finn insists that the reception must take place inside the majestic underwater kingdom. He explains that Leah and Jeremy will be in one special bubble while their respective families will be in another special bubble.

Both individuals will be enclosed in unique bubbles, witnessing awe-inspiring underwater shows and performances. Finn reveals that the royal family is already aware of my uniqueness, and your own family recognizes it as well deep down. Share this information with your family discreetly and privately, and they will surely accept it. Jeremy embraces Finn and expresses excitement about showcasing these mesmerizing underwater performances to everyone.

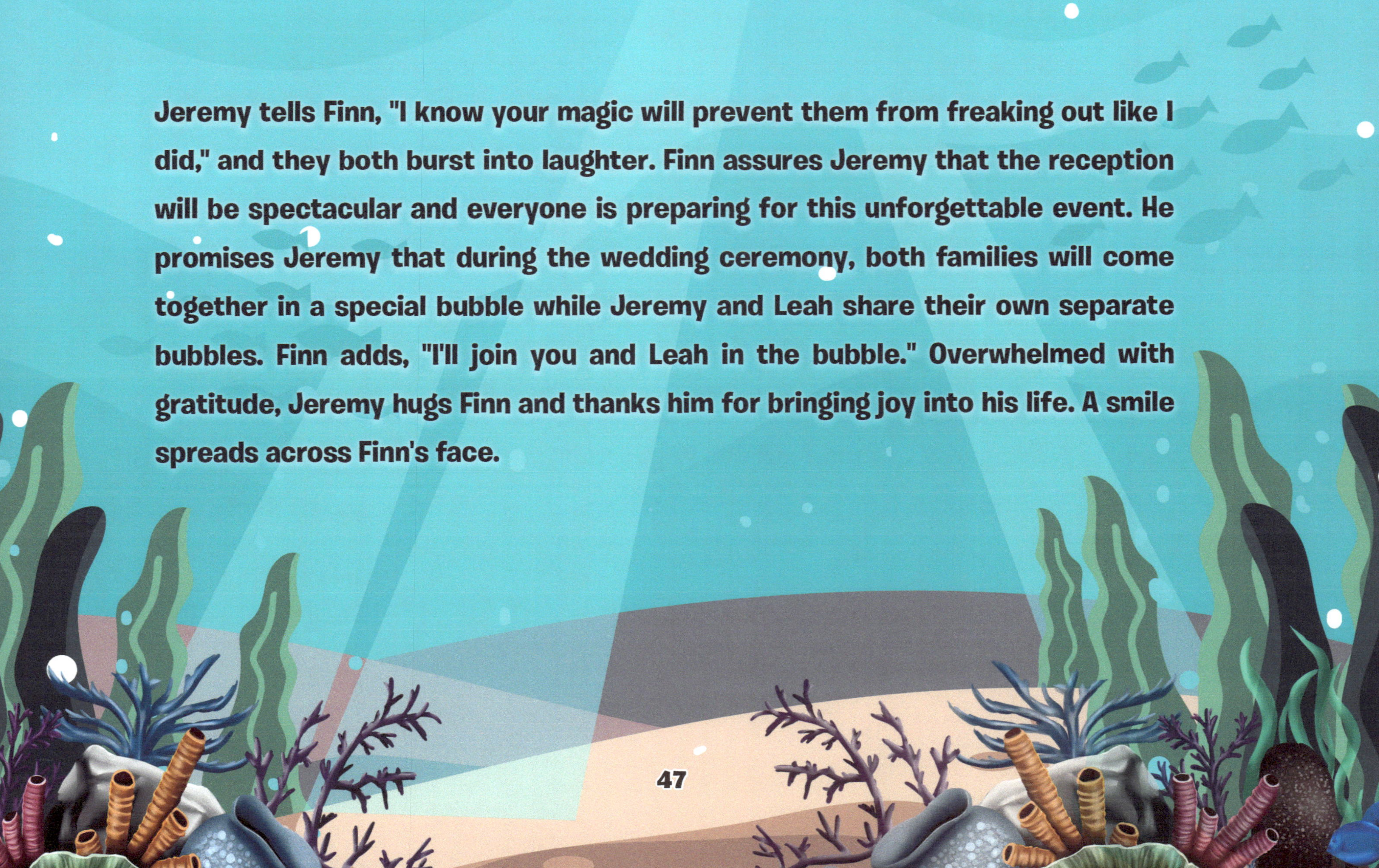

Jeremy tells Finn, "I know your magic will prevent them from freaking out like I did," and they both burst into laughter. Finn assures Jeremy that the reception will be spectacular and everyone is preparing for this unforgettable event. He promises Jeremy that during the wedding ceremony, both families will come together in a special bubble while Jeremy and Leah share their own separate bubbles. Finn adds, "I'll join you and Leah in the bubble." Overwhelmed with gratitude, Jeremy hugs Finn and thanks him for bringing joy into his life. A smile spreads across Finn's face.

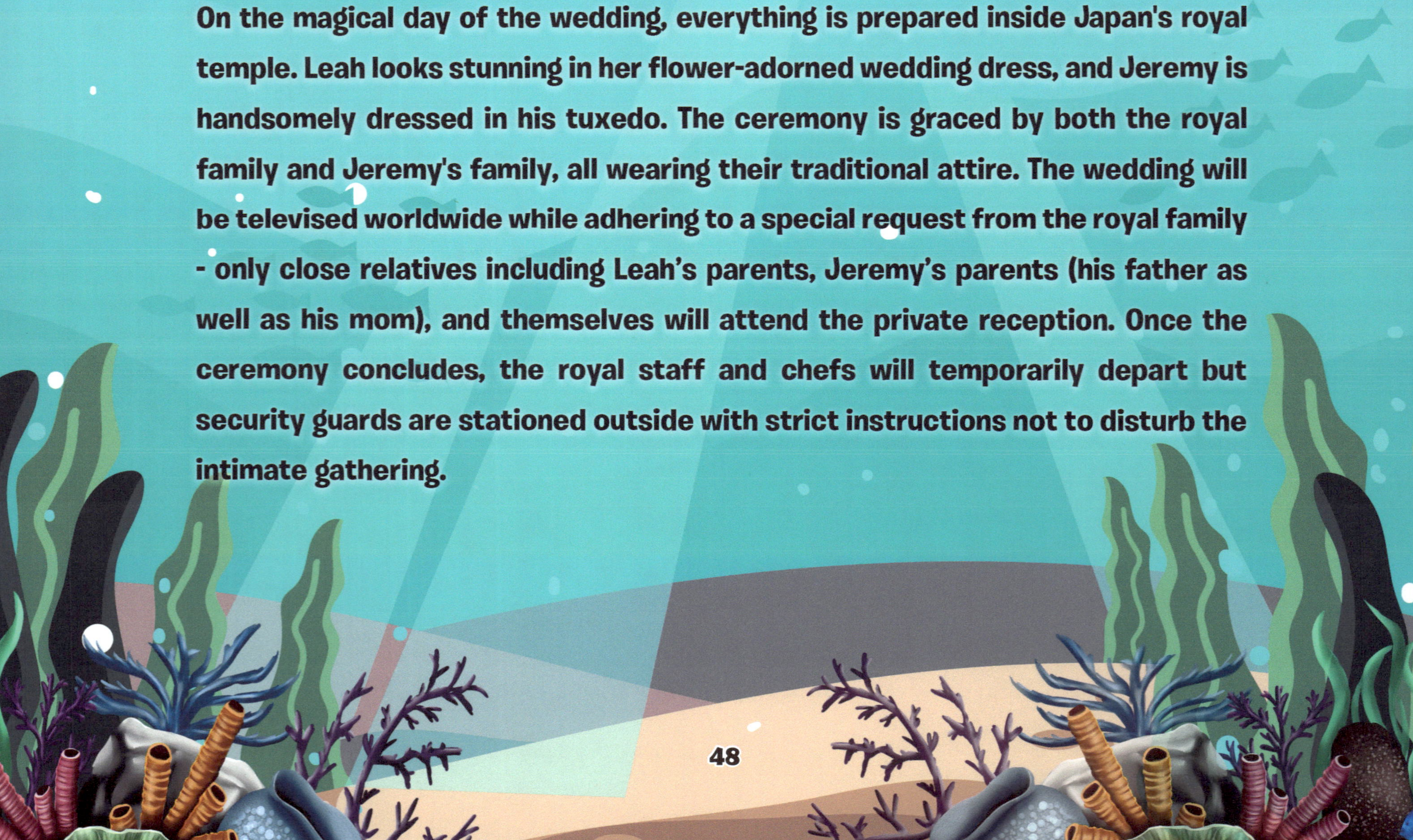

On the magical day of the wedding, everything is prepared inside Japan's royal temple. Leah looks stunning in her flower-adorned wedding dress, and Jeremy is handsomely dressed in his tuxedo. The ceremony is graced by both the royal family and Jeremy's family, all wearing their traditional attire. The wedding will be televised worldwide while adhering to a special request from the royal family - only close relatives including Leah's parents, Jeremy's parents (his father as well as his mom), and themselves will attend the private reception. Once the ceremony concludes, the royal staff and chefs will temporarily depart but security guards are stationed outside with strict instructions not to disturb the intimate gathering.

As the wedding began, there was an enchanting atmosphere. Leah and Jeremy looked absolutely stunning as a couple, captivating viewers through their TVs and radios. Joy and love filled the air as the royal priest conducted the ceremony while Raymond's Navy comrades stood by; they would depart after this momentous occasion. The significance of hosting a private wedding reception is understood by all - it honors age-old traditions in the royal family that involve solely immediate relatives. Finn, nestled within his ancient cubic aquarium, delightedly joins Carol and her mother for this special celebration. As hours go on, congratulations are exchanged with hugs, handshakes, and plans made for gatherings throughout the week: invitations to dinners and other events ensue.

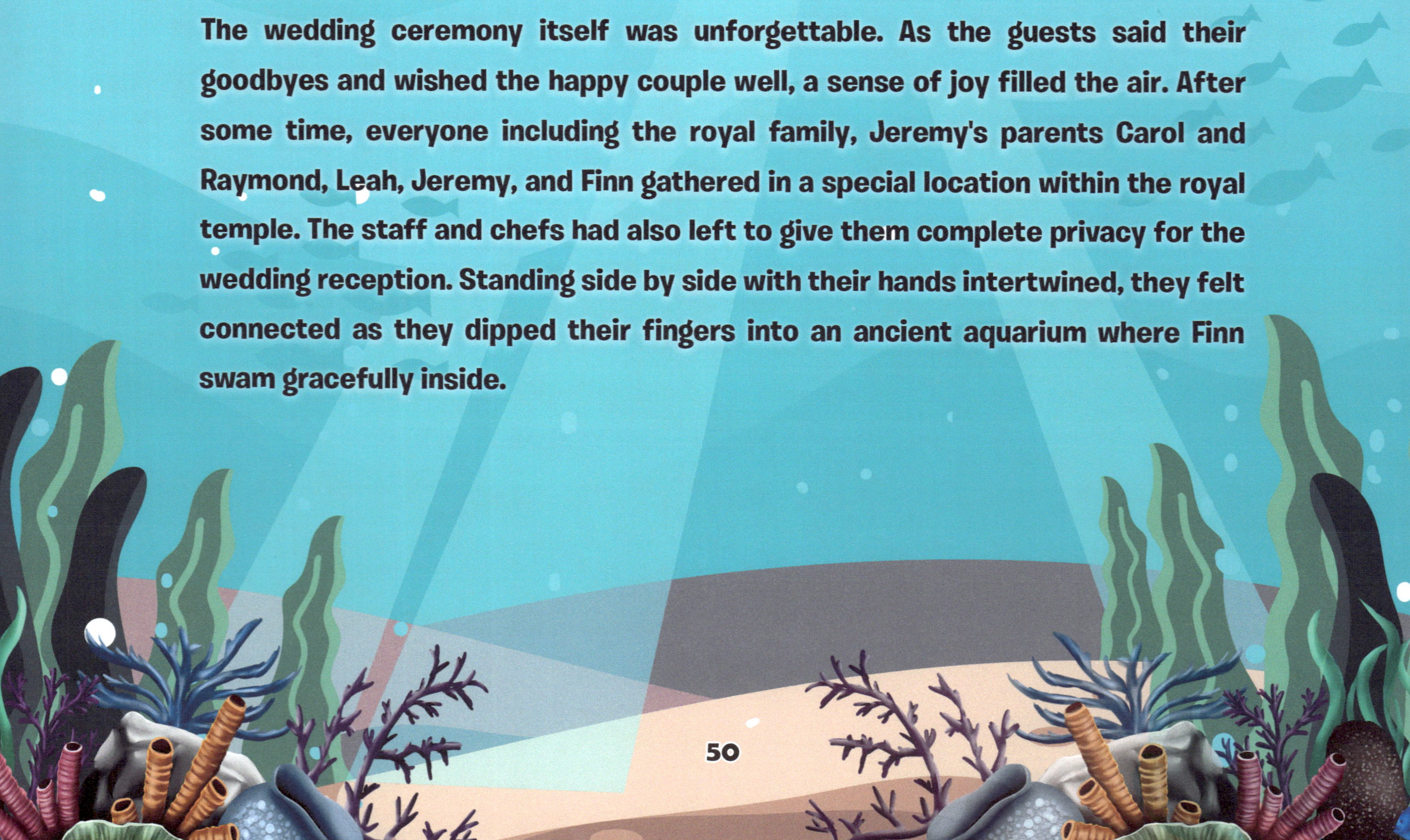

The wedding ceremony itself was unforgettable. As the guests said their goodbyes and wished the happy couple well, a sense of joy filled the air. After some time, everyone including the royal family, Jeremy's parents Carol and Raymond, Leah, Jeremy, and Finn gathered in a special location within the royal temple. The staff and chefs had also left to give them complete privacy for the wedding reception. Standing side by side with their hands intertwined, they felt connected as they dipped their fingers into an ancient aquarium where Finn swam gracefully inside.

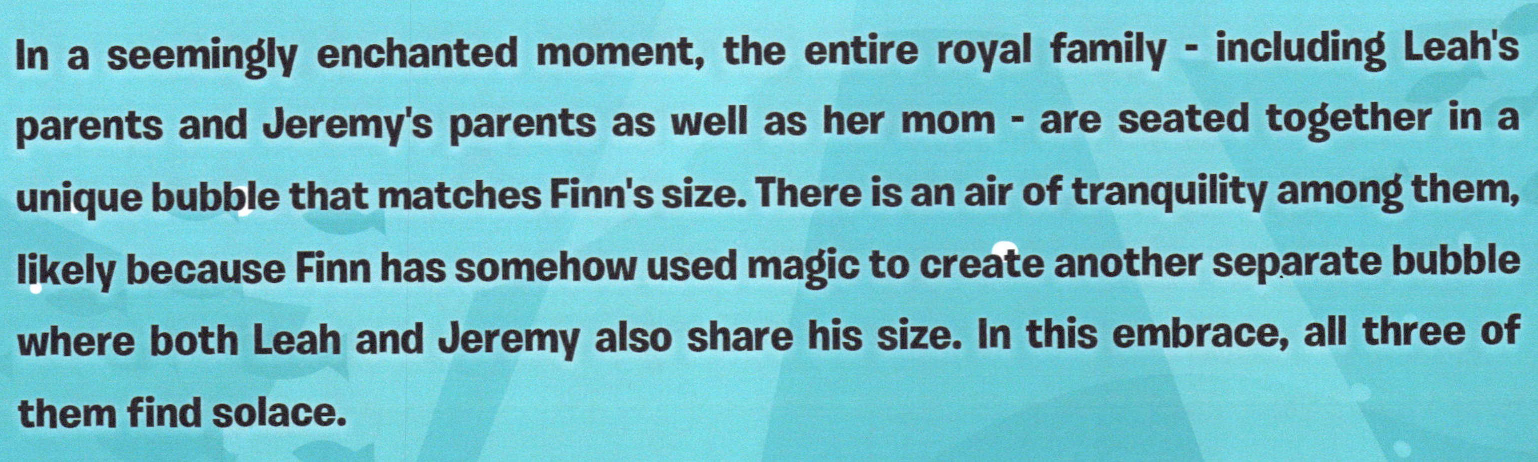

In a seemingly enchanted moment, the entire royal family - including Leah's parents and Jeremy's parents as well as her mom - are seated together in a unique bubble that matches Finn's size. There is an air of tranquility among them, likely because Finn has somehow used magic to create another separate bubble where both Leah and Jeremy also share his size. In this embrace, all three of them find solace.

They find themselves submerged underwater, transported to an enchanting kingdom beneath the sea. They are surrounded by a multitude of fish, all gathered inside a grand seashell auditorium that is filled to capacity. The crowd eagerly waves at them as they await the commencement of extraordinary aquatic performances. Suddenly, the octopus symphony orchestra begins playing under the direction of their maestro, filling the surroundings with harmonious melodies that resonate everywhere. Each instrument is skillfully played in perfect harmony. Both the royal family and Jeremy's family are utterly captivated by this awe-inspiring sight, and Leah and Jeremy along with Finn share in their amazement. Next, hundreds upon hundreds of squids emerge from hiding writing "welcome" using their remarkable ink capabilities–a truly surreal spectacle to behold!

MAJESTIC UNDERWATER
KINGDOM

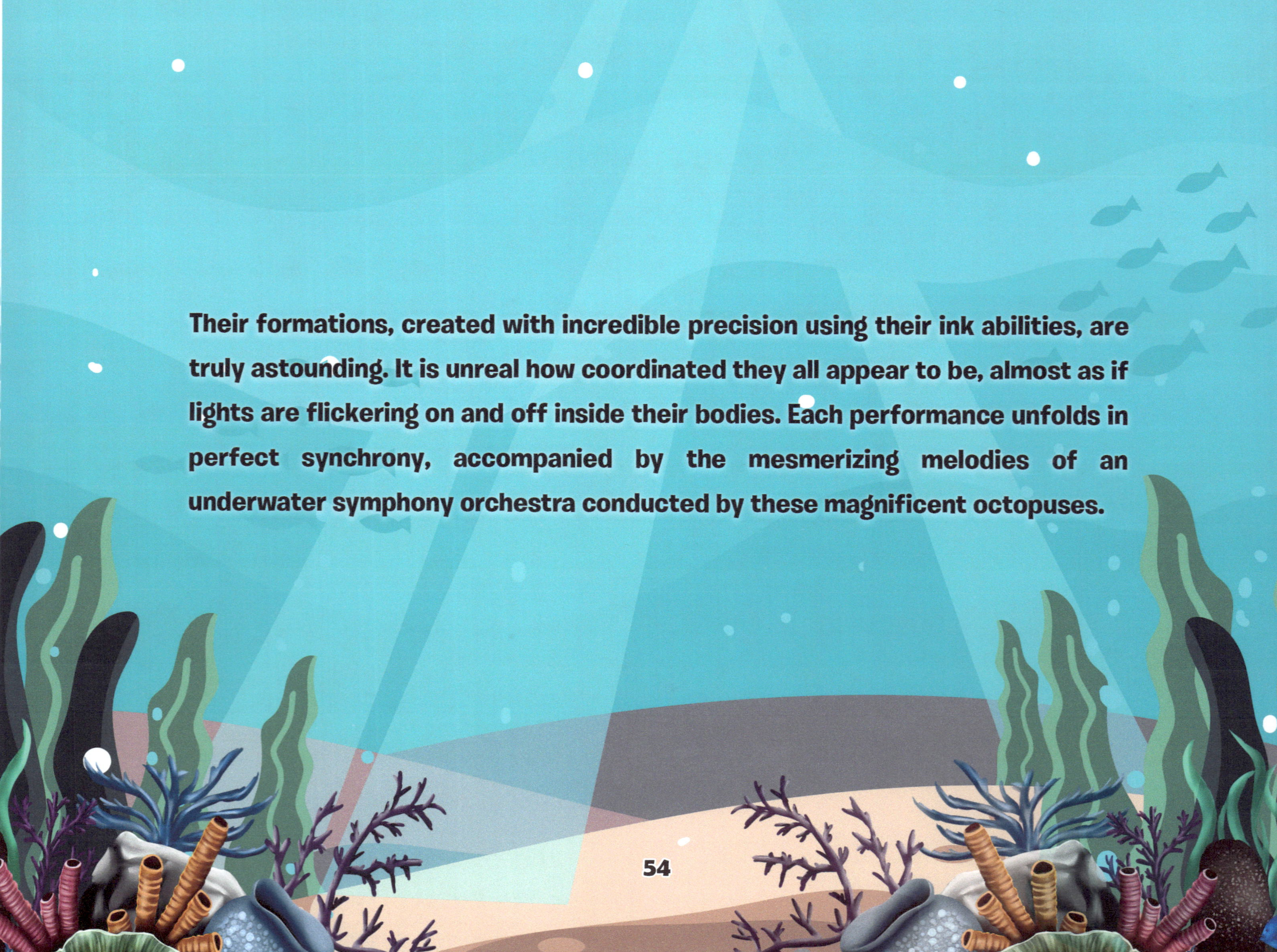

Their formations, created with incredible precision using their ink abilities, are truly astounding. It is unreal how coordinated they all appear to be, almost as if lights are flickering on and off inside their bodies. Each performance unfolds in perfect synchrony, accompanied by the mesmerizing melodies of an underwater symphony orchestra conducted by these magnificent octopuses.

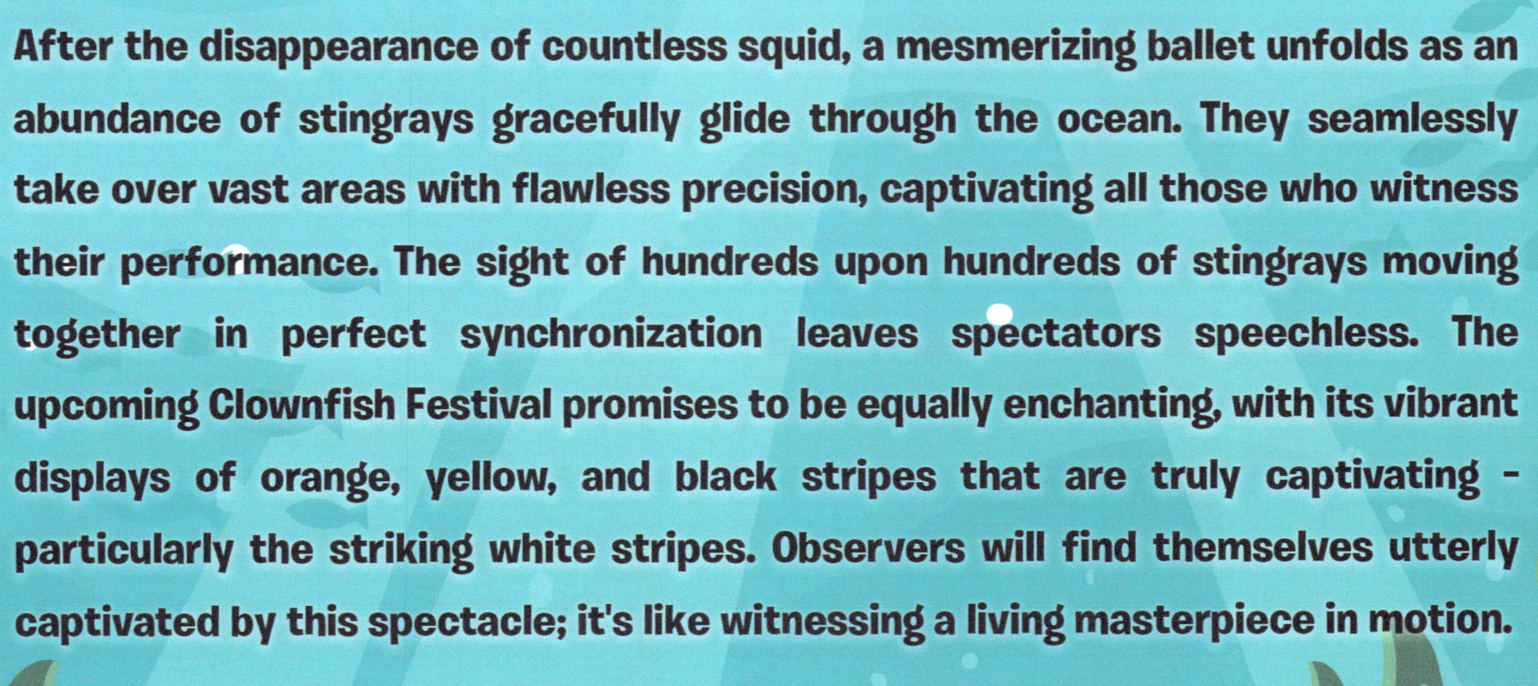

After the disappearance of countless squid, a mesmerizing ballet unfolds as an abundance of stingrays gracefully glide through the ocean. They seamlessly take over vast areas with flawless precision, captivating all those who witness their performance. The sight of hundreds upon hundreds of stingrays moving together in perfect synchronization leaves spectators speechless. The upcoming Clownfish Festival promises to be equally enchanting, with its vibrant displays of orange, yellow, and black stripes that are truly captivating - particularly the striking white stripes. Observers will find themselves utterly captivated by this spectacle; it's like witnessing a living masterpiece in motion.

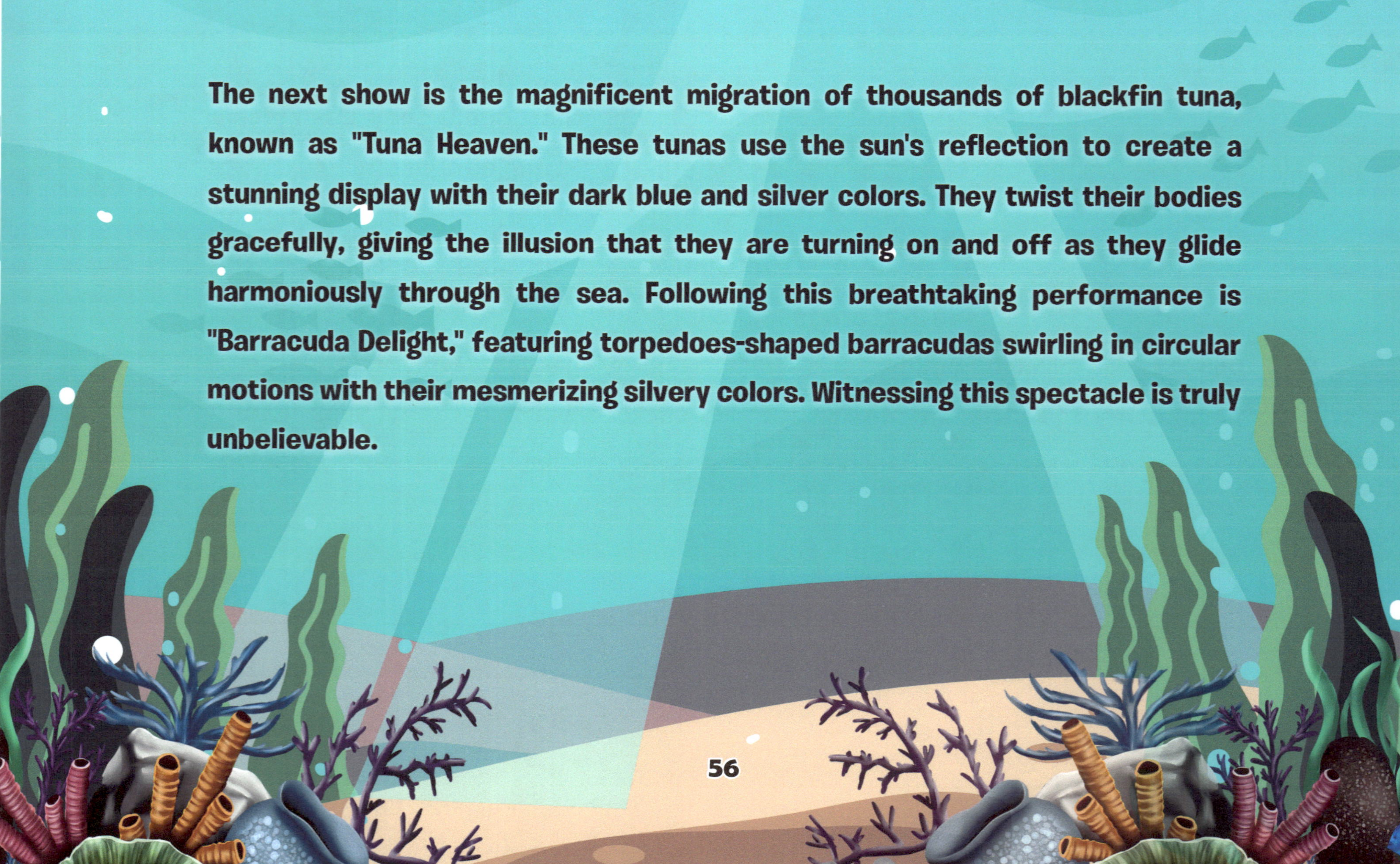

The next show is the magnificent migration of thousands of blackfin tuna, known as "Tuna Heaven." These tunas use the sun's reflection to create a stunning display with their dark blue and silver colors. They twist their bodies gracefully, giving the illusion that they are turning on and off as they glide harmoniously through the sea. Following this breathtaking performance is "Barracuda Delight," featuring torpedoes-shaped barracudas swirling in circular motions with their mesmerizing silvery colors. Witnessing this spectacle is truly unbelievable.

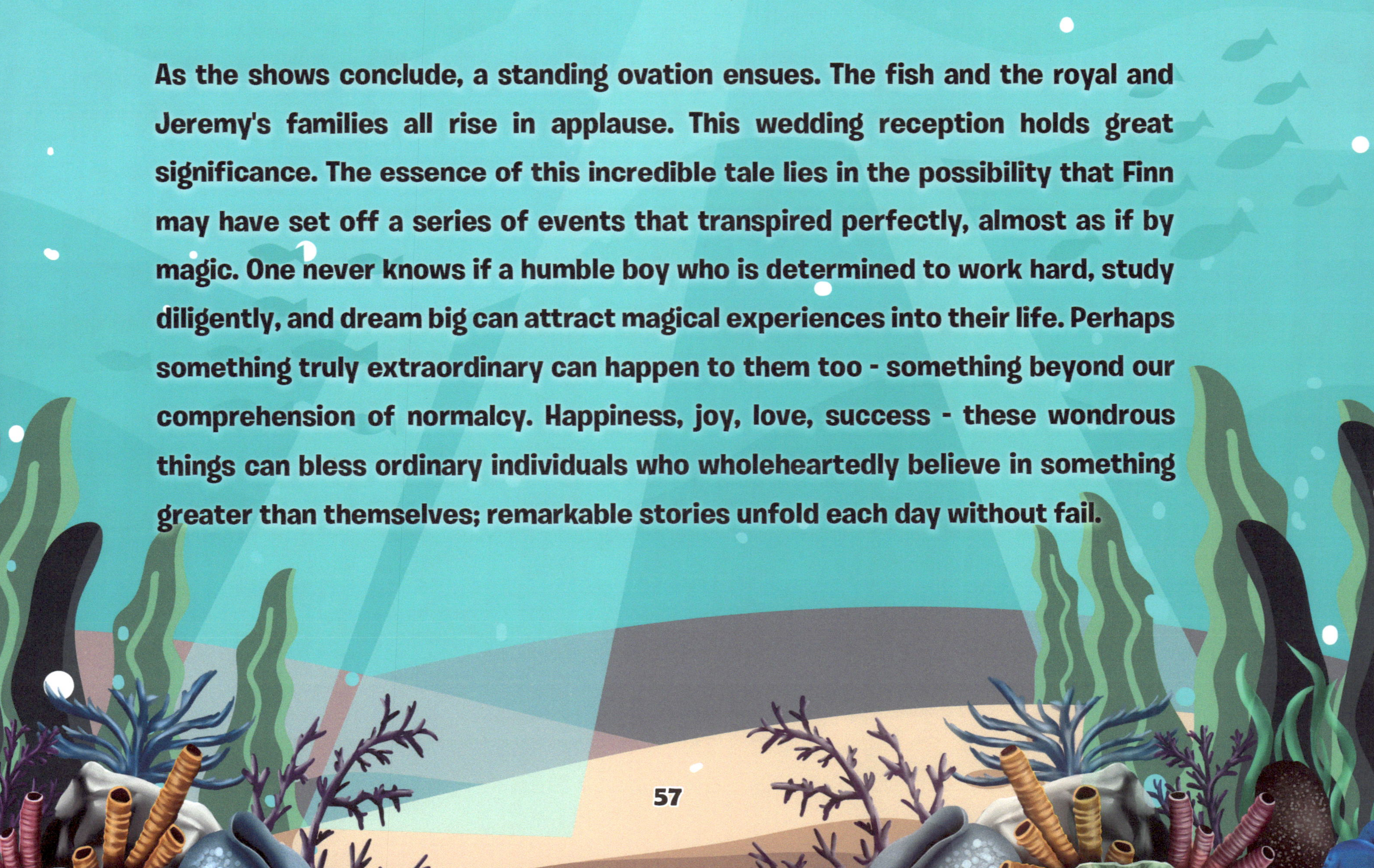

As the shows conclude, a standing ovation ensues. The fish and the royal and Jeremy's families all rise in applause. This wedding reception holds great significance. The essence of this incredible tale lies in the possibility that Finn may have set off a series of events that transpired perfectly, almost as if by magic. One never knows if a humble boy who is determined to work hard, study diligently, and dream big can attract magical experiences into their life. Perhaps something truly extraordinary can happen to them too - something beyond our comprehension of normalcy. Happiness, joy, love, success - these wondrous things can bless ordinary individuals who wholeheartedly believe in something greater than themselves; remarkable stories unfold each day without fail.